HURRICAMP!

HURRICAMP!

Steph Katzovi

BROWN BOOKS KIDS

Hurricamp!

Brown Books Publishing Group
Dallas, TX/New York, NY
www.BrownBooks.com
(972) 381-0009

A New Era in Publishing®

Publisher's Cataloging-In-Publication Data

Names: Katzovi, Steph, author.
Title: Hurricamp! / Steph Katzovi.
Description: Dallas, TX ; New York, NY : Brown Books Kids, [2022] | Interest age level: 007-012. | Summary: "Ten-and-three-quarter-year-old Laura "Noodle" Newman had high hopes about going to sleepaway camp for the first time. Once she's there, however, Noodle is miserable. No one can help her get over her terrible homesickness ... As a menacing hurricane heads up the coast, life at Camp Hillside turns upside down. Through the craziness, Noodle realizes that only one person can make her feel better: herself"-- Provided by publisher.
Identifiers: ISBN 9781612545547 (paperback)
Subjects: LCSH: Camping--Juvenile fiction. | Homesickness--Juvenile fiction. | Hurricanes--Juvenile fiction. | CYAC: Camping--Fiction. | Homesickness--Fiction. | Hurricanes--Fiction. | LCGFT: Humorous fiction.
Classification: LCC PZ7.1.K3746 Hu 2022 | DDC [E]--dc23

This book has been officially leveled by using the F&P Text Level Gradient™ Leveling System.

ISBN 978-1-61254-554-7
LCCN 2021923082

Printed in the United States
10 9 8 7 6 5 4 3 2 1

For more information or to contact the author, please go to www.StephKatzovi.com.

To all those who love—or wish
they loved—bug juice.

Chapter 1

THE ADVENTURE BEGINS

Thump! My stomach began to lurch with every bump. And there were plenty of bumps as we drove down the winding gravel road. Our silver SUV was so full of stuff that it felt like the bottom of the car might scrape against every speed bump that we rumbled over.

"There it is!" my father said with a little too much enthusiasm as we drove up to the front gate. He was the only one talking this morning, more than making up for the silence coming from my mom and me. I looked to where he was pointing. The sign was supposed to say, "Camp Hillside, a place for girls and young women adventurers," but I had noticed that some of the letters were faded. Like the "w" in "women." That was definitely a bad omen.

"You getting excited, Noodle?" my dad asked. He glanced over his shoulder as we hit another bump. I tried to nod, but the seat belt cut into my neck whenever I moved my head. I noticed my mother was dabbing at her eyes again. Her usual chatter about, "Remember this," and, "Don't forget that," stopped once we'd shoved my bulging trunk into the car this morning.

1

The curved road that led to the camp seemed to go on for miles. The speed bumps had been replaced by random dips in the worn pavement. The bouncing did not help my stomach. Camp Hillside wasn't exactly in the middle of nowhere, but it sure felt like it.

"Look, there's the Great Lake!" my father exclaimed, wildly gesturing to a large mossy green body of water in the distance. I wanted to talk, but the words caught in the bottom of my throat. It didn't matter. My dad hardly noticed that he was having a one-way conversation. "I'm sure Jill wishes she could be in two places at once. Right, Sandy?" my dad asked. He looked over at my mother, who had silently pulled out another tissue. My mom, Sandra Newman, is a teacher at Great Falls Middle School, and my dad, Harvey—or Dr. N. as he's called by his patients—is an orthodontist. Jill's my big sister by three-and-a-half years.

Jill was the Camp Hillside veteran in our family. She had promised over and over that she would be there for me at camp. But this year, Jill was invited to spend the entire summer in Italy with Lucia. Lucia was the exchange student she'd become best friends with last year. Jill could barely speak Italian.

For the next four weeks, Camp Hillside would be my home. All by myself. Away from my parents, my sister, and all my friends. In other words, away from everyone I knew and loved.

By the looks of the dried patches of grass and rustic wooden cabins, this place had been frozen in time for many summers. I looked around and tried to guess where I was going to. All I could see was one hill after another. I guess that's how Camp Hillside got its name.

I wondered which cabin was for the Sandpipers. That was my bunk. I hoped my bunkmate was nice. It would be great if she liked all the same things as me. I loved sports, music, and writing (but not always in that order). Even if we were a little different, I imagined that we'd become instant best friends. I had really high hopes for camp . . . right up until I was actually supposed to go to camp.

When our car stopped in the parking spot, I looked at the huge stretch of land that surrounded me. I suddenly saw sleep-away camp through a different pair of eyes. I wasn't just "one of the Newman's" or "Jill's sister" anymore. *I* was the camper. I tried to tell myself that everything would be fine. Jill always talked about how great camp was all year. There had to be some reason for that. Screams and laughter in the distance brought me back to reality. Suddenly, every sound bugged me.

As I climbed out of the backseat and wiped a bead of sweat from my upper lip, I prayed that camp wouldn't be that bad. Then, I glanced over at my mother.

"Well . . ." my mom started to say. She couldn't get any other words out. She turned away again, wiping tears from her eyes. We'd barely gotten out of the car before two muscular young men came to collect my belongings. At the same time, a tall woman with honey-blonde hair and a giant straw hat bounded over to greet us.

"Hello, Newmans!" the woman said. The two guys picked up my trunk and walked away with it. "I'm sorry Mom and

Dad, but to help our campers and staff foster a community of teamwork and trust, families must say their goodbyes here." This was how we'd dropped off Jill for the past three summers, but both of my parents looked stunned. I guess because they'd never dropped off their youngest (and favorite?) child.

"Yes, of course. Nice to see you again, Dotty," my dad said with fake cheer. Dotty directed the camp with her husband, Bob. Dotty, who was very tall and reminded me of a flamingo, gave my parents a brief hug before looking at me with her big, toothy smile.

"I'm sure you'll love Camp Hillside just as much as your big sister, Miss Newman," Dotty said. She gave my shoulder a squeeze. Dotty glanced at a car pulling into the space right next to ours, and said, "Duty calls!" Then she dashed over to the next family. She repeated the same line about saying goodbyes from this awful, dusty parking lot. My parents turned to me with forced smiles.

"We'll miss you, kiddo," my dad said with a sniffle. He quickly wiped his eyes and began fiddling with something in the trunk. I blinked my eyes furiously, trying to keep my tears inside.

"Goodbye, my baby. I'll miss you," my mom said as she dabbed at her eyes again. "I'm sorry, Noodle. I didn't want to cry in front of you. It's just hard to let my baby girl go." She paused for a moment and took a deep breath. "Oh, but you're going to have so much fun. I love you," my mother said, her voice trembling. "I love you so very much." Well, I think she might've said something like that. At that point, I totally blacked out. All

I could hear was a voice in my head saying, "This is it. Mommy and Daddy are leaving you."

"We should go, Sandy. Let's let Noodle get settled in and all," my father said quietly. My mom nodded and showered me with tons of kisses. No number of kisses would be enough to get me through the next four weeks.

As soon as my parents said their sniffly goodbyes, it was like someone had flipped a switch. The distant laughter stopped. The skies turned gray. The pit in my stomach felt like it swallowed up my whole body. Any excitement I had felt about camp vanished. I had made a terrible mistake. I didn't actually want to go to sleepaway camp! Not now. Maybe not ever. I wanted to be with my parents. I didn't care that they were going to help Grandma Gert move into a new apartment in boiling-hot Florida. At that moment, I would have gone just about anywhere with them . . . except for carpet shopping or picking out bathroom tiles. Those are two of the most boring things in the world.

"Don't leave me!" I shouted. I would've run after their car, but a gentle hand guided me in the opposite direction.

"Hi, there! You're Noodle, right? Welcome to Camp Hillside! Welcome to the Sandpipers' bunk! I'm your counselor, Shelby," a young woman said. I couldn't reply because she just kept talking. Her sunny personality was paired with wavy, reddish-brown hair. She had a constellation of freckles. "You're about to have the *best* summer of your life! Let's catch up with the rest of the 'Pipers. Everyone is super excited to meet you."

I highly doubted that. For a second, though, I believed her. We had to walk for ten minutes up at least six hills. I saw a bunch of girls sitting on a picnic table when we finally got to the cabin.

"Should I put my stuff away first?" I asked. I was nervous that my trunk might've been delivered to the wrong cabin.

"Don't worry about your things just yet, Noodle," Shelby said. She sensed my concern. "We'll make sure you get set up in just a moment. Since you're the last to arrive, you can pop into the bunk right after we say our hellos. I've got some great name-games to try out!"

"Sandpipers, gather around me over here," Shelby said. She added in an ear-splitting whistle to make sure she had our attention.

"What are we doing?" a petite girl asked. Her unwrinkled outfit was the exact opposite of mine.

"I'm about to tell you," Shelby said. Once we all made a lopsided circle, she announced "Okay ladies! Pop a squat," and motioned to the ground. I had never heard the phrase "pop a squat" before. What was a squat? Was it a tiny, furry troll? Or was it more like a bug? If you popped one, would its guts spurt all over and make a huge mess? I looked around to see if there were any of these "squat" animals around until I realized that Shelby wanted everyone to sit down. I quickly sat down in a pile of dirt instead of on the grass.

"Okay, Sandpipers," Shelby said with a laugh. "Let's start off with some introductions." Shelby slapped her hands on her lap twice. Then she clapped once. She repeated the slap-slap-clap pattern so that it sounded like a steady drumbeat. *Slap-slap-clap, slap-slap-clap.* I looked at Shelby curiously. The other girls quickly figured out that they were supposed to join in before I caught on.

"Let's make getting to know each other fun," Shelby said. She continued her slap-clapping. "I'll start. My name is Shelby," she slap-clapped to the beat. "And I'm from Texas. I'm your counselor . . . and I like breakfast." I noticed that "Texas" and "breakfast" didn't really rhyme. But Shelby talked with a Southern accent. She pronounced breakfast like "break-fiss."

The girls kept up the rhythm. Shelby explained, "So, tell us your name, where you're from, and something interesting about yourself. Let's start with you, Holly." Holly had blonde hair. She wore Camp Hillside gear from her headband down to her socks. Something about her rubbed me the wrong way. I wasn't quite sure what it was.

"My name is Holly, and I'm from Richmond." Holly paused for a moment before resuming her beat. "And my favorite nut . . . is an al-mond."

"Nicely done, Holly," Shelby said. She gave an encouraging nod. "Okay, Tara! You're next." Tara had braces that sparkled in the sun when she smiled or laughed, which was a lot. Tara was eager to show off her slap-clapping skills. I could tell by the way she copied Holly that the two were close friends.

"Okay, here goes," Tara said confidently. She led the group in slap-clapping. "My name is Tara, and I'm from the South. I've got lots of metal things . . . in my mouth." Tara pointed to her teeth to show off her colorful braces. The girls—mostly the ones who had been to Camp Hillside before—laughed loudly.

"Well done, well done!" Shelby said, clapping her hands enthusiastically. "Okay, you're next," Shelby said. She pointed to a girl with tight lips and a furrowed brow.

"Oh, I'm not really good at this kind of stuff," the girl said shyly.

"That's okay! Just give it your best shot," Shelby said, nodding her head in encouragement. "We're all friends here . . . or at least we will be at the end of the next four weeks!"

"Come on, Charlie," Holly said, glancing at the girl. "You can use whatever you said last summer."

"Umm, I don't exactly remember what I said . . . but okay," the nervous girl said. "My name is Charlie," she slap-clapped awkwardly. "I'm from the East. I like to bake . . . and sometimes I use yeast." Charlie didn't have the rhythm—or the attitude— that Holly and Tara had. She breathed a sigh of relief when her turn was over. She seemed nice. Maybe she was someone I could be friends with.

"Very good, Charlie," Shelby said. "Now, how about you?" Shelby pointed to a tall, lanky girl.

"Watch out!" the girl said with a grin, "Because this is going to be good." Wow! She was confident.

"My name is Buffy," she said, slap-clapping like she'd done this a million times. "I'm from New York. And y'all can tell . . . that I'm no dork!" When she finished, Buffy giggled, put her hands on her hips—even though she sat on the ground—and wiggled her head from side to side like one of those bobblehead dolls. All the girls laughed. Even I couldn't help but smile.

"That was *awesome*," Shelby said. She sang the word "awesome" like she was in a choir. I tried to remember all the girls' names after their introductions. As Shelby moved around the circle, I found it hard to keep them all straight. It was also getting harder to keep up the slap-clap beat. My hands were kind of tired. Shelby pointed to a red-headed girl, who was small and wore the same fashionable outfit as Holly and Tara.

"Oh, is it my turn?" she asked. It was like she had just sat down and was trying to figure out what was going on. I saw Tara mouth the word "airhead" to Holly.

"Okay," the girl said with a deep breath. "Here goes."

"My name is Janice," she slap-clapped. "I'm from Montclair. Everyone knows me . . . by my hair." Janice pointed to her hair and announced, "It's red!" just in case anyone could miss her flaming red hair.

"I love both the rhyme and the hair," Shelby said, pointing to her own head of red hair. "Alright, we've got three more girls to introduce." Shelby pointed to the girl sitting on my right. That meant I was next. In all the time people had introduced themselves, I hadn't been thinking of a rhyme for myself. Suddenly I wished I'd come from a better hometown. There wasn't a lot that rhymed with Great Falls: halls, malls, brawls, shawls, walls . . .

What else rhymes with Great Falls? Think, Noodle, think! I was only half-listening when the girl sitting next to me began.

"My name is Marla," she began. "I'm from Pleasant Valley . . . and my younger sister's name is Sally." Holly and Tara looked at Marla with raised eyebrows.

"Well, actually, that's not true," Marla admitted sheepishly. She saw Holly and Tara staring at her. "My sister's name is Stacy. I just couldn't think of anything that rhymed with Valley."

"It's okay!" Shelby said. She smiled tenderly. "Remember, this is just for fun. We're getting to know each other!"

"We're down to two," Shelby said, "so how about you?" She pointed to me. She cackled hysterically because she rhymed "two" with "you." I started slap-clapping and hoped a rhyme would pop into my head. It didn't. The girls in the circle shifted in their seats. They stared at me impatiently.

"My name is Laura," I began. I quickly lost the beat. "Umm, but people call me Noodle." *Oh, golly. This isn't going well.* I tried to get back in rhythm, but I slap-clapped too quickly. I clapped half a beat off and blurted out, "Okay, my name is Noodle . . . I'm from Great Falls . . . and I like sports you play with balls."

"That's super! Thanks, Noodle," Shelby said. She spoke with such enthusiasm that I felt like I just came up with the best rhyme in the history of this awful game.

"Okay, last but certainly not least," Shelby said. She looked at a thin, pale girl with frizzy, black hair. It was as dark as a raven. She was busy plucking a piece of grass.

"Whatever," the girl said glumly. She half-heartedly slap-clapped. "My name is Aries . . . and I'm from who care-ies."

Shelby looked at Aried with surprise, as if it were impossible that someone did not love to rhyme while also keeping time with their hands.

"Come on, Aries," Shelby said. She looked at Aries with a pretend pout.

Aries breathed a dramatic sigh. "Fine. My name is Aries," she began again. This time she was perfectly in rhythm. "I'm from the Island . . . and someday I'm going to Thailand." Aries folded her hands in her lap as soon as she was done.

"Fantastic!" Shelby said. She was back to her happy self. "That was super. You guys totally rocked the introductions!" Some of the girls shared high fives. Nobody offered a hand to me. My heart sunk deeper in my chest. I saw a dandelion and plucked the yellow top off its stem. It fell from my fingers and disappeared into a patch of long grass. I watched an ant climb up and down over the dandelion before disappearing into an anthill. I wished I could just disappear, too.

Shelby continued with the icebreakers. She seemed like she was enjoying them the most. As for me, I went from feeling bad to worse. The lump in my throat grew bigger by the minute.

"Um, can I take a look around the cabin?" I asked. I didn't want everyone to see me cry. Visiting the bunk seemed like a perfect excuse. We were interrupted by a high-pitched scream.

"Janice, what's the matter?" Shelby asked. She hurried over to Janice and her fiery red hair. Janice clutched her arm.

"I got stung by a bee!" she shrieked. This was the perfect opportunity for me to escape.

I ran into my oversized trunk as soon as I walked through the cabin door.

"Great! I'll be first in line for all the mosquitos Jill warned me about," I muttered. I sighed and tucked my brand-new solar system blanket over my bunk. The bed let out a huge *creak!* as I buried my face in my pillow. I could still smell my mother's perfume on the pillowcase. It soon became damp from my tears. I don't know how long I had been crying. Suddenly, I felt a shadowy presence standing over me. I looked up and saw Aries right next to my bed. She'd come at the worst possible time.

"Hey, I'm Aries. Like I said in that awful name-game. I'm the top bunk," she said. She pointed to the bed over my head. I didn't say anything. She shifted her feet uncomfortably. She didn't make eye contact. When I saw her there, so pale and uneasy, I wanted to cry even more. It wasn't that Aries didn't seem nice. Who knows? She probably was. She looked almost like a porcelain doll against her black T-shirt and dark jean shorts. She didn't look like she enjoyed spending time in the sun. She didn't seem like she enjoyed much of anything.

"Hi," I said mid-sniffle. "I'm Laura, like I said—well, *tried* to say—before. But everyone calls me Noodle." Aries nodded awkwardly. A fat tear rolled down my cheek.

"How did you get the nickname Noodle? It doesn't sound anything like Laura," Aries asked. She respectfully ignored my runny nose.

"Well," I began. I tried my hardest not to sniffle. "When I was around two years old, my big sister, Jill, and I were eating pasta one night. My mom says that I pointed to Jill's plate and then pulled at my hair and said 'Noodle.' I had just started talking. Maybe my parents thought I was a genius or something. After that, the nickname sort of stuck."

"That's a cute story," Aries said without any emotion. She shifted on her feet again. I don't think she knew how to handle my tears.

"Yeah, I guess," I said. I casually wiped my nose with my arm. It left a wet trail in its wake. I knew I was making an awful first impression with everyone. I just felt so miserable. Aries' eyes followed my every move.

"You know . . ." Aries said softly. It was like she didn't want anyone else to hear her. "If you live in three-day chunks, you'll make it to the end of the first session easily." I looked up at her. Did she have the cure for my awful case of homesickness?

"It's worked for me," Aries continued. "And I should know. I've been to so many camps . . . there was Camp Chitaqua, Camp Silver Springs, Camp Happy Times, Camp Roscoe Lake . . ." Aries listed each camp name and counted them out on her fingers. "There's more, but they all blend together after a while. And let me tell you . . . Camp Happy Times was anything but happy." Aries shrugged. I wish I told her how grateful I was for her advice. Instead, I just said something stupid.

"Well, maybe Camp Hillside will be the camp you end up liking," I said. But I knew that neither of us ever wanted to come back.

"Yeah, maybe," Aries said. She flipped her dark hair. She didn't seem hopeful. "Well, I'll let you get back to your . . . whatever," she added. I don't think she knew where to take the conversation from there. Aries climbed up to the top bunk. She tried to read for a bit before my crying drove her back outside. After a while, I needed a break from crying. I decided to write my parents a letter.

Sunday, June 28

Dear Mom, Dad, and Grandma Gert,

I am using one tissue for my left eye and one tissue for my right eye to wipe away the tears while I write. I used the same tissue for my nose all day. It's soggy and about to tear. I will probably need to throw that one away pretty soon. Maybe I'll hang it outside to dry and I can use it again. I don't know if I'll have enough tissues to last me for four weeks. I hate sleepaway camp. The room is too dark. My bed is too creaky. I'm pretty sure the bathroom has spiders in it.

Also, I don't like the girls in my cabin. My bunkmate, Aries, seems more grumpy than friendly. One girl named Charlie said she liked my soccer jersey, but then she started talking to some of her old camp friends and never came back. Another girl named Janice was friendly, but she kept calling me "Ziti" instead of Noodle. She may not be the brightest crayon in the box, if you know what I mean.

There are some other girls, but they basically ignored me. I forgot their names anyway.

I know I wanted to try something new this summer by going away to camp, but I've changed my mind. Please come and get me as soon as you read this letter. Grandma Gert, I'm sure you will understand.

Sealed with snot,
Your sad daughter (Noodle)

I finished the letter in my neatest left-handed penmanship. There were plenty of smudges on the paper. I laid back down and cried some more. I would have stayed on my creaky bed for the next four weeks. But then Shelby came into the room and interrupted my pity party.

"Hey, you," Shelby said. She looked at me with a sad smile. "There's a welcome pep rally down at the Sports Field in a few minutes. Let's get some fresh Camp Hillside air into those lungs of yours." I didn't move. Shelby delicately grabbed my arm and guided me outside. "It's a bit of a hike from here, so we'll need to get moving." Shelby's gentle-but-firm tone indicated that I didn't have a choice. My feet somehow moved me forward.

"Noodle, Aries, Buffy," Shelby said, motioning to the three of us. "You guys come hang with me. I'll give you the fifty-cent tour of the camp on our way to the pep rally." Since we weren't sitting in a circle, I could see that Buffy was a tall and lanky girl. Seriously: she had abnormally long legs. She might have even

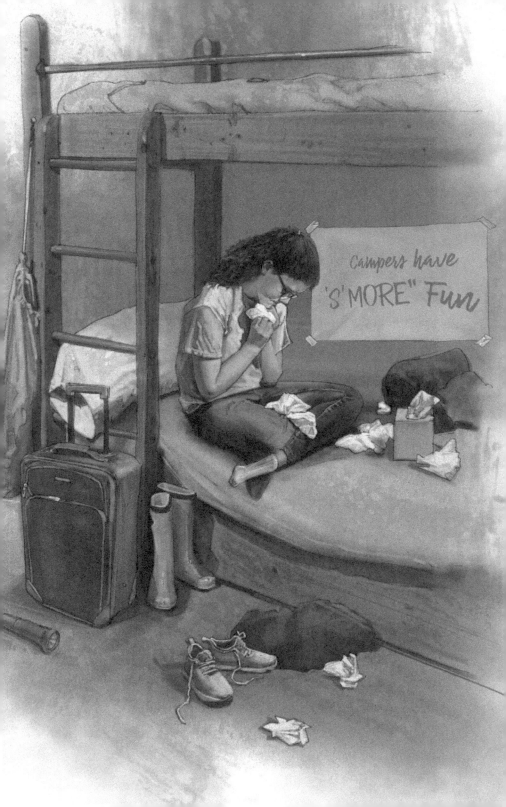

been scary if she didn't have such a wide smile and eyes that seemed to laugh, even when she didn't say a word. She wore a tomato-red shirt that said, "Awesome Ends With 'Me!'" I liked it. I think Buffy and I would have been friends if this wasn't one of the worst experiences of my life.

"Great shirt, Buffy," Shelby said. It was like she read my mind. She pointed to Buffy's T-shirt. Buffy grinned from ear to ear.

"Which way is the Trading Post?" Buffy asked. She rubbed her hands together eagerly. "My cousin said you could buy lots of candy there."

"I'll point it out when we pass by," Shelby said. "But I'm sure your parents wouldn't want you to go overboard. Gotta make sure you have your fruits and veggies, right?" Shelby playfully punched Buffy on the shoulder.

"Do they have *fruit* candies here? That should work," Buffy said. She laughed. Shelby made friendly conversation as we walked. She did her best to help us new girls feel better, but Shelby's charm only worked on Buffy. Buffy already looked very comfortable. She laughed and joked with Shelby. The rest of the Sandpipers chattered away. They made up for lost time since last summer. Tara and Holly sang silly cheers as they walked along.

"We've got spirit, yes we do!" Holly shouted. Her shiny teeth sparkled. Her blonde hair was pulled into a perfect ponytail. Holly ignored me after she saw my swollen eyes and runny nose. I soon figured out that Holly made herself the leader of the Sandpipers.

"We've got spirit, how 'bout you?" answered Tara. She was clearly Holly's loyal sidekick. Tara was almost identical to Holly. She was just slightly taller. A rainbow headband held back her brown hair. Tara's hair was braided in a fancy fishtail braid. I secretly admired it. My style was made up of a plain ponytail, basic clothes, and thick glasses. It was no match for their fancy hairstyles and coordinated outfits. I couldn't copy them even if I tried.

Tara might be nice, but only when she wasn't around Holly. On the long walk to the Sports Field, I watched their hair swing back and forth with each step. It was almost as if their hair was dancing.

"How long can you two goofballs keep that up?" Charlie jokingly grumbled. I had high hopes for becoming friends with Charlie. But then she sat down next to Holly and Tara. That ended it for me. Shelby motioned for the rest of the Sandpipers to sit down next to her on a patchy spot in the grass.

"Janice! Janice, over here!" Shelby waved to one of our bunkmates. She had somehow joined a younger group of campers.

"Those girls did seem a little bit small," Janice said as she plopped down. She nearly sat on my lap. "Sorry," Janice added. She gave me a small pat on my knee. I smiled and shifted over politely. The camp directors, Bob and Dotty, stood on a small, creaky stage. It looked like it was moments away from collapsing. They motioned for everyone to sit down.

"Welcome to Camp Hillside!" Bob yelled into the microphone. He had a bushy white beard and reminded me of a summertime Santa Claus. He was a little too loud, and the microphone let out a piercing *screech*! I cupped my hands over my ears. Charlie had also covered her ears. She gave me a quick smile when she saw me making the same face. Okay. Maybe she wasn't so bad after all.

I barely paid attention to Bob and Dotty as they rambled on about the rules. We couldn't bring food into the cabins. We had to make sure not to wander off. Most of the rules seemed pretty obvious. I needed to remember the rhyme for when you're trying to figure out if a plant is poison ivy. If you see a suspicious plant, think, "Leaves of three, don't touch me."

"But most of all, ladies!" Bob shouted. His voice shocked me into focusing on his words. "Let's have some fun!" Everybody around me cheered. They danced to the music Dotty had put on. I glanced around. Nobody else looked homesick. They all seemed perfectly happy. Aries didn't seem as happy, but she didn't really seem to care. Not me. Never in my ten-and-three-quarter years of existence had I ever felt so sad and alone. I decided that nothing else in my life was worse than sleepaway camp. Not even having strep throat last winter, which was awful.

Chapter 2

NOTES FROM NOODLE

The days after the pep rally were a blur. On Tuesday, I thought it was Wednesday. I didn't realize my mistake until lunchtime on what I thought was Friday. It was only Thursday. It felt like someone had secretly changed the calendar that dangled from a rusty nail on the wall by my bed. It didn't really matter what day it was. I walked around in a fog and felt sorry for myself almost every day.

The swim test was soon. I rifled through my trunk and pulled out a new blue one-piece bathing suit. It had three stars spread across the top and onto one shoulder strap. I felt like a member of the Olympic swim team. I glanced around to see everyone else's bathing suits. They had on brightly colored bikinis or tankinis with fringe. I felt plain and boring once again. We all put on enough sunblock to make Shelby happy. She led us out of the cabin like she was the head of a marching band.

"Give me your left, left . . . left, right, left!" she shouted cheerfully. Shelby walked quickly to her beat. The Sandpipers shuffled along behind her. We came to a huge lake at the edge of a clearing.

"There she is," Shelby said. She proudly pointed to the greenish-brown water. "Camp Hillside's own Great Lake." The lake was large. But it wasn't that impressive. One of the swim instructors saw Shelby and shouted, "Here comes the Counselor of the Year!" Shelby's freckled cheeks turn red. They almost matched the color of her red hair.

"That's Kurt," Shelby whispered to Buffy, Aries, and me. "All the counselors call him Kurt the Flirt."

"He's so cute," Holly said. She stared at Kurt dreamily. Kurt was tall and muscular. He had sandy brown hair and twinkling green eyes. I was no expert, but even I could see that he was good-looking.

"All right, Sandpipers," Shelby said. Her cheeks had returned to their normal color. "We'll go alphabetically *backwards* for the swim test. Tara, Noodle, Janice, and Marla! You guys head over to Kurt first. Everyone else will hang out on the beach until it's the next group's turn." I looked at what Shelby called the "beach." Were we looking at the same place? All I saw was a small plot of sand. It could've been mistaken for a dirt pile if there wasn't a sign that said "Beach" right next to it. *I don't think anyone will visit this beach on their next family vacation,* I thought. A pang of homesickness washed over me as I looked back at the murky lake.

I guess it's sink or swim around here until you figure out what's going on. Pun intended, I added to myself. I would have laughed if I were in a better mood.

"You girls ready to get in the water?" Kurt asked. "I heated it up for you this morning. Just jump right in!" Kurt motioned to the water with a laugh. I didn't want to be the last one in. I leapt off the edge of the dock.

"What is she do—?" was the last thing I heard Marla say before I plunged into the ice cold water.

Marla, Janice, and Tara went to the ladder at the edge of the dock. I had foolishly decided to follow Kurt's advice and jump in.

"Ahhhhhh!" I shrieked when I came back up to the surface. Janice and Tara were still dipping their feet in the water from the ladder. As I gasped for air, I didn't feel homesick. Instead, I felt mad.

"Why didn't anyone tell me how cold this stupid water is? Why didn't anyone tell me I wasn't *really* supposed to jump in? Why is everyone so happy when camp is so awful?" I shouted. Even though I was the only one in the freezing water, everyone else looked frozen as they stared at me. They were either shocked at my outburst or surprised that I was dumb enough to jump in the water.

"Aw, Noodle, I'm so sorry," Kurt said. He tried to pull me out of the water. "I didn't think anyone was going to jump in. But good for you! You've got spirit."

"Noodle, do you want to do the swim test another time?" Shelby said. She had sprinted over from the beach.

"No," I said, with a sniffle. "I'm already in the water. I'll do it now." Somehow, I pulled myself together and went through with the swim test. Even though I accidentally drank a little lake water at the end, I felt like I did okay on my strokes and at treading water.

When we had all finished our tests and were warming up on the dock, Kurt congratulated us on doing such a great job. "Noodle, you might just get swimmer of the summer," he added. He smiled broadly right at me.

"Here are your swim levels until we test again in two weeks," Kurt said. He passed out small pieces of yellow paper to everyone. I looked down and saw that my paper had first said, "*Perch.*" That word had been crossed out and replaced with, "*Barracuda.*"

"Ooh! Barracuda," Charlie looked at my paper. "That means you don't need swim lessons." I glanced up at Charlie. I tried to smile the best smile I could muster. It was nice to not need swimming lessons. *But I'm not planning on staying at Camp Hillside for much longer,* I thought.

I would have spent the entire week in our cabin if I had the choice. I just wanted to stare at the room around me. I counted the eight creaky bunkbeds over and over. I stared at the buttons on an old radio. Shelby turned it on every afternoon for the Camp Hillside radio broadcast. I studied every knot in the wood on the walls. I memorized every crease and crinkle. I even noticed the tiny water spot on the poster next to my bunk. The poster said, "Campers Have 'S'more' Fun." This was clearly not true.

Nothing could break me out of my funk that first week. The daily "check-ins" with Bob and Dotty or the "friendly" walks that Shelby took me on didn't help. Not even the mounds of mail that I had received made me feel happy. The only thing that made me feel better was writing. I wrote my parents a letter every day . . . sometimes I would write them more than once. I would also write to Grandma Gert. I hoped she would share the messages with my parents.

Saturday, July 4 or Sunday, July 5 (?)

Dear Grandma Gert,

Hi again. I got your last letter. I'm glad that there is a swimming pool in your new apartment complex. Speaking of swimming, we just got the results back from our swim tests. I'm a Barracuda, which means I'm one of the top swimmers. Did my parents tell you that the lake at camp is GROSS? It's called the Great Lake. There's really nothing great about it.

There are tons of leaves in it. The water is freezing. I learned that the hard way. The swim instructor told us to jump right in because the water was warm. So I jumped. But he was only teasing! My counselor Shelby calls him "Kurt the Flirt." The water was _freezing_, and I got really mad. Everyone laughed _at_ me, even though they said they were laughing "with" me.

I really don't think tests should be allowed at camp. Maybe we could test out new ice cream flavors. But every flavor would get a passing grade. Except for coffee ice cream. It tastes disgusting even when you cover it with whipped cream and sprinkles. I'm sorry if that's your favorite flavor . . . but I'm pretty sure you love chocolate.

Oh! There's a girl named Marla in my group. She complains even more than the ladies you play cards with. Her dad wrote a note to the camp that said, "Marla has an ear infection all summer and can't swim in the lake." You should ask Daddy to write me an excuse that says the lake water is bad for my teeth.

Okay, well, the girls will be back from jewelry making soon. Can you please ask my parents to send more stamps and more tissues ASAP?

With love and cold, dirty lake tears,

Noodle

When I didn't want to explain how awful camp was to my parents and Grandma Gert, I wrote in my journal. It was a blue spiral notebook. I wrote "Noodle Newman" on the cover in giant bubble letters. I wanted everyone to know that it was mine. I had written down the camp's daily schedule on page three. It made me feel a little better to write out the plan for the day.

☑ 7:00 am – Wake up

☑ 7:25 am – Breakfast line up + Reveille (pronounced "REV-uh-lee." It's some French word. I think it means, "Wake up.")

☑ 8:30 am – Cabin clean-up

☑ 9 am – Activity #1

☑ 10:05 am – Activity #2

☑ 11:10 am – Activity #3

☑ 12:30 pm – Lunch

☑ 1 pm – Siesta/mail call

☑ 2 pm – Cabin activity

☑ 3 pm – Snack

☑ 3:10 pm – Activity #4

☑ 4 pm – Optional Rec (*or check-in with Bob + Dotty)

☑ 5 pm – Shower Hour (*can just splash water on face if
    went swimming)

☑ 6 pm – Dinner line up/Lowering of the Flag

☑ 6:45 pm – Trading Post + Evening Activity

☑ 9:20 pm – Lights out

Shelby made me do everything on the schedule even when I said I was tired. I almost always said I was tired. I knew that Shelby meant well. But I just wanted to go home. I would have even gone to Florida with my parents! Bob and Dotty said I should try to be positive and think of the best parts of each day. There were only two positives during that first week. The first was playing soccer. The second was the excitement leading up to our first Radio Hillside broadcast.

Radio Hillside was the camp's radio station. It was everyone's favorite channel. It was also the only channel that came in clearly. Everyone was excited for their chance to talk on the radio. Camp Hillside had fourteen cabins. Each one could go on air at least twice in a session.

I was super excited to go on Radio Hillside. I could come up with better material than everyone else I had heard. But I would never admit that out loud. Most campers only said "hi" to their friends or screeched into the microphone.

"Ladies! We visit Radio Hillside today," Shelby said on Friday morning. The girls cheered. I would probably hear that same screaming when we were on air later.

I had never been to Radio Hillside before. I had only seen it in the background of a photo of my sister Jill. I imagined Radio Hillside was a big, modern building. I thought it would have a huge beacon on top, with red blinking lights. Boy, was I wrong. Radio Hillside was basically an old, run-down shed. The only way I knew we were in the right place was because of the neon sign in the window that read "Radio -illside." The H had probably burnt out long ago and had never been replaced.

When we got inside, we met a nice guy named Clay. He was the sound engineer. Clay wore a beaten-up baseball hat backwards. He spoke with a slow southern drawl.

"Since this may be your first time on air," Clay said, "Let me give you a run-down of the rules." Because of Clay's accent, "on air" sounded like "on err." He listed off the rules, "Don't press any buttons. Keep things positive and PG—no swearing." I'm pretty sure none of us listened to what Clay said once we saw the giant microphone and headphones in the radio booth.

"Oh, this is going to be so much fun," Holly said. She took the words right out of my mouth.

Chapter 3

ARIES' CHANGE OF PLANS

Holly and Tara started fighting over who would go on the air first.

"I think we should go on in alphabetical order," Charlie suggested. That was a great idea if your name was Aries, Buffy, or Charlie.

"How about *reverse* alphabetical order?" Tara said. She made sure to say "T-t-t-tara!" in case we didn't realize her name came up first.

"Sandpipers, listen up," Shelby said. She got everyone's attention with the loudest whistle I'd ever heard. "We have thirty minutes on the air. There are eight of us. I'm splitting you up into three groups so you all have enough time to talk and play some music. Each group will have ten minutes on the air."

"But thirty divided by eight is . . ." Aries paused to calculate the math. ". . . Three point seven-five minutes per person," she said with a satisfied nod. "How will the timing work?" Shelby was waiting for this question. Maybe she had been a counselor at Camp Hillside long enough to know how to divide up a thirty-minute time slot with minimal fighting.

"We'll split up. There will be three people to a group. One group will have two people," Shelby said. She paused while Aries did the math in her head. Aries nodded in approval after a moment. "We'll draw names out of a hat." Shelby motioned for Clay's baseball hat. It looked like it had never been washed. He shrugged and handed it over.

Pick me, pick me, pick me, I thought as Shelby fished around Clay's hat. She pulled out three names: Marla, Janice, and Holly. *Darn it!*

"Ladies, remember the rules," Clay said. He looked right at Holly for an extra second. Holly didn't notice his stare. She was too busy writing down the songs she wanted him to play. They spent the first three minutes and forty-nine seconds saying hi to everyone they knew. That seemed like a huge waste of time. But I'm sure that Miss Rosa, the chef from the Mess Hall, was happy for the shout-out. Buffy, Charlie, and Tara went next. They weren't much better than Marla, Janice, and Holly. Buffy stood too close to the microphone. Every "p" she said made a loud popping sound.

"Who's feeling haPPy out there today? SandPiPers, are you feeling haPPy?" Buffy asked. The listeners obviously couldn't answer. It just sounded like Buffy, Charlie, and Tara shouted to themselves. It goes without saying that they were terrible, too.

"Aries and Noodle, you girls will close the show!" Shelby said excitedly. The second group was almost done. I couldn't tell if Shelby was trying to make us excited. She might have been happy to be close to done with this activity. I didn't care.

My heart was beating so fast. I couldn't wait to get up to the microphone. Then Aries ruined things. She got stage fright.

"You know what? I think I just want to help run the controls," Aries said. Her eyes darted nervously toward the booth as Buffy, Charlie, and Tara walked out noisily. We had less than a minute before our turn. Shelby looked at Clay. He shook his head no.

"Aries, just try to go on air for now," Shelby said quietly. Clay glanced at the big clock on the wall before he quickly pressed a button. That queued up another song.

"Sorry. We can't have dead air," he explained.

"But I *really* don't want to go on the air anymore," Aries said. Her face looked even paler than normal. Clay looked at Shelby, unsure of what to do. Shelby glanced at the empty sound booth and then back at Clay as if to say, "Oh, jeez."

"Noodle, maybe you just go on by yourself for today?" Shelby offered. "Aries, how about you just sit next to Clay this time?" Aries nodded slowly. She looked relieved.

"Can Tara and I go again?" Holly asked. She stepped right in front of me. "Just to keep Noodle company for her very first time on air," she added. She drew out each word slowly. There was a fake smile plastered on her face.

"That's a nice suggestion, Holly. We're going to let Noodle have her own turn. I'm sure she'll be great!" Shelby said. She casually blocked Holly's path and guided me to the booth.

"Just a time check for y'all. There's about five minutes left before Afternoon Rec ends," Clay said when I put the headphones on. The excitement I had felt before suddenly turned sour. "Actually, there's only about four minutes left. I'll try to stretch the time out if I can. The pre-programmed music goes on automatically at two-thirty. I'm really sorry, Noodle." Clay started his "three-two-one" countdown before I could respond. The red light suddenly went on. I was on-air. Everyone stared at me and waited for me to speak.

Chapter 4

MISERY WITHOUT COMPANY

I panicked. All I could think about was how little time I had. Four minutes? What could I do in four minutes? I probably lost thirty seconds while I thought about how little time I had. Maybe I could do just one bit from all the material I had prepared? I patted my pockets. I frantically looked for my papers. Today was not the day to forget my notes!

"Uhhh," was the only sound that came out of me. Clay urgently tapped a finger on his mouth, signaling for me to say something. I glanced at Holly. She was laughing at me. I could hear her cackle even from behind the glass. She grabbed her neck and turned to Tara. She pretended she was choking. I couldn't see Buffy or Charlie, but I noticed that Marla was laughing too. There was nothing I could do. I was frozen. I heard Clay put on another song. Then I heard the closing music. When I finally came to my senses, I ripped off the headphones and stumbled out of the booth. I had blown my four minutes of fame.

"I'm really sorry, Noodle," Aries said. She wrung her hands. "I panicked. I feel awful that it messed things up for you. You can have all my time when we come back here." I nodded my head slowly. I felt absolutely miserable. Shelby was the next one to offer her consolations.

"You'll be the first to go on the next time we're on air. No matter what," she promised. Buffy and Charlie also offered their apologies. Holly, Tara, and Marla, however, didn't say anything. I was positive they were still making fun of me. That made me feel even worse. Boy, I really didn't like them.

Shelby didn't force me to join the next activity. It was archery. It would have felt good to hit something, but the quills from the arrow gave me blisters. I was happy to skip it. I went back to the cabin and wrote another letter to my parents and Grandma Gert.

Thursday, July 9

Dear Mom, Dad, and Grandma Gert,

I hope you are having a nice time in Florida. How was your July 4th? We had a barbeque with lots of red, white, and blue foods. There were lots of blueberries. Is it hot there? It's been raining here just about every other day. I still don't like camp. I hope Bob and Dotty told you that, too. I asked them to call you.

I don't really think I can make it until the end of the first session. I just bombed on Radio Hillside. I literally froze when it was my time to talk. I guess I should be thankful that it was only radio, and no one saw me? That's pretty much all the news I feel like sharing now. Tune in tomorrow for my next awful installment . . . once I write it.

Signing off with sniffles,
Noodle

I only felt a little better after I finished my letter. I decided to write to my sister. She should know how awful I felt, too. After all, it was pretty much her fault that I was alone at Camp Hillside.

Dear Jill,

I wanted to say hello. I don't know if I'll have enough stamps left to mail you another letter. I bet you're having a great time in Italy. You're probably eating lots of pizza and spaghetti. Mommy and Daddy dropped me off almost two weeks ago. I have hated every second of camp. I remember you said I was going to "love, love, looooove camp." I don't.

My bunkmate Aries said that she has seen campers who are way more homesick than me. Bob and Dotty probably have, too. Aries also overheard our counselor tell Bob and Dotty that I'll get over being homesick if I "power through." I don't know how Aries gets all this information. I do know that she did NOT become my best friend like your bunkmate did.

Well, camp isn't amazing and wonderful like you said it would be. I hope you're having fun with Lucia and her family.

I'll see you in August . . . if I haven't shriveled up into a sad little raisin by then.

Love, Noodle

Now my whole family knew how miserable I was. But it didn't matter. Everyone I loved was too far away to save me. I wanted to show the people at camp that I was more than the sad, homesick girl. I wished they could see the real me. They needed to see the person that all my friends, neighbors, and teachers knew and loved. Maybe tomorrow. *Maybe tomorrow things will finally get better. I'm really going to try and be happy tomorrow. I swear.*

Chapter 5

BUG JUICE FOR BREAKFAST

"You take the fastest showers ever, Noodle," Shelby said. She put the day's mail on everyone's beds later that afternoon. She noticed I was writing in my journal again. "I hope that's for the next time we're on Radio Hillside."

"It is," I said. I tried to remember a funny joke I had come up with at lunch. I couldn't wait to get back on the radio to prove myself to everyone.

"Good! We'll be back on the radio in a few days . . . you'll see. The time will fly by," Shelby said. I'm sure she was happy that I was no longer crying or staring at the cabin walls. And I couldn't disagree. Nobody likes a "wet Noodle," after all. "Wow! Look at all the stamps on this letter that came for you," she added. She handed me my mini stack of mail. I spotted an Italian postmark. It was a message from Jill. Finally! I tore the envelope open. I nearly ripped the paper inside.

Dear Noodle,

Fingers crossed you get this letter before camp is over. The mail is sooooo slow in Italy. It is beautiful here and the food is amazing. I do miss everyone. Yes, even you! ☺

I hope you are having a blast. I bet everyone loves how funny and clever you are. I can't wait to hear all your stories. I'm sure you have a million by now. Wasn't I right when I told you that all the flavors of bug juice are gross?

I have so much to tell you when I get home, but I need to get something off my chest. I was too embarrassed to tell you before I left. As you know, sometimes it's easier to say things in writing then in person. So here goes . . .

My first time at camp, I was so homesick. Like crying nonstop, miserable-all-the-time sad. Dotty pulled me aside on one of my worst days. She told me, "Take a twenty-four-hour break from feeling sorry for yourself." I told her I would try. When I looked at all the people around me, I saw that I was the one who was missing out. After that, I stopped waiting for Mom and Dad to get me. I learned how to do things on my own. Camp got easier. Then my life became non-stop fun.

Even though Italy is awesome, I wish I could be in two places at once. Please promise me that you will remember every second of Camp Hillside. You have to tell me everything when we're back in Great Falls.

Okay, it's time for dinner. The pasta here is so yummy! See you when I see you.

xoxo and LYLAS (Love You Like A Sister—because you are!)
Jill

Jill had been homesick too? How could she not tell me? Had I been too young to know? Still, I couldn't believe my camp-crazed sister started out just like me. It would have been nice to hear Jill's story before I left. Maybe Jill didn't want me to think differently of her.

I'll be honest. I didn't wake up the next day or even the day after that totally homesick-free. But things started to slowly get better each day. I had finally settled into a routine. I had tons of ideas for my next time on Radio Hillside.

It took me about ten days to go from feeling fully miserable to semi-miserable to "sort of okay." Then things started to get interesting around camp.

Shelby and the rest of the girls in my cabin burst through the door during Shower Hour one day.

"It is so windy outside!" Holly yelled.

"Yeah, it's definitely ponytail weather," said Tara. She always agreed with Holly.

"Did anyone have the bug juice at lunch today?" Janice asked. She tripped over the cabin steps and stumbled into the room. "It was redder than my hair!" She pointed at her head.

"I had the bug juice. It was disgusting . . . as usual," Marla answered loudly. She never wanted to be left out. We were used to hearing Marla's opinions. We had lived with her for almost two weeks. Sometimes Marla could be really funny. I don't think she tried to be funny on purpose, though. Marla had shared her strange thoughts about potatoes earlier that day.

"Potatoes are, like, the hardest working vegetable," Marla had said. "They make fries, pancakes, and chips. They even can be used as stamps for arts and crafts. They're a much worthier vegetable than, like, spinach. What can a piece of spinach do?" We all laughed at that comment. Sadly, Marla's opinions were more annoying than amusing most of the time.

"Marla, you complain all the time. Do you even like anything? You don't like the bug juice. But you still drink it. Every day," Charlie said. She rolled her eyes. "Be careful! You might turn into a bug." Everyone giggled when Charlie lightly pinched Marla like bugs were biting her.

"Ouch!" Marla shrieked as if Charlie had attacked her. "Well, I'm just hoping that the bug juice will be good one day," Marla answered. She pouted. "It looks like it should taste good, doesn't it?"

"Umm . . . no!" Buffy roared. She let out a deep belly laugh. She was wearing a shirt that said, "Give Peas A Chance." It had a picture of smiling green peas. If anyone asked me, I would have gladly shared my opinion on bug juice. Like Marla, I expected it to taste delicious. The one day I tried it, I was very disappointed. Bug juice is tangy and sweet at first, but it has a gross, chalky aftertaste. After that, I decided to stick with the always-delicious chocolate milk. I would have thought about chocolate milk a little longer if Shelby hadn't cleared her throat.

"Ladies, I have something a bit . . . urgent to discuss with you. Let's gather over here for an official cabin meeting," Shelby said. She motioned to a worn-out rug in the middle of the room. It probably had a million years' worth of dust on it. We all scrambled to find a spot. By the time Aries and I made it over, there was just a small sliver of rug left for us.

"So, I've got some good news and some not-so-good news," Shelby began when we were all seated.

"Give us the bad news first . . . then it will be out of the way!" Marla shouted. I'm pretty sure Marla preferred the bad news just so she could have something to complain about.

"No, give us the good news first. That way, the bad news won't seem so bad," Tara said. She glanced around at the others for their approval. Her ponytail nearly whipped me in the face.

"Just to save time, we are not going to take a vote," Shelby said. She knew that we could easily spend the next twenty minutes fighting over whether she should share the good news or bad news first. "Okay, so . . . a big storm is about to hit the southern tip of Florida," Shelby said slowly. This news quickly made Marla and Tara quiet down. They had still been fighting over which order was best to receive Shelby's news.

"It *was* the bad news first," Marla whispered. She gave a happy nod. Shelby was too focused on her speech to pay attention to Marla.

"We're going to the Mess Hall for a special meeting with Bob and Dotty in a few minutes," Shelby said. She spoke in a serious voice that I had never heard from her before. I didn't like this side of Shelby. "The weather forecasters predict that the storm will head north in a few days. That means it will be coming closer to us. We should be totally fine here at camp, but I, uh . . . think Bob and Dotty should give you all the details."

"Are you talking about Hurricane Hilda? The big storm that's all over the news?" Aries asked. How would Aries know about a hurricane in Florida? Radio Hillside didn't have the news or weather reports. The only news we could get came through the mail. And Aries didn't get much mail.

"Wait, what? There's a hurricane? And we *should* be fine?" Buffy asked. Her eyes bulged wide. Staying calm during emergencies was not one of Buffy's strengths. I thought her behavior was ironic. Buffy had worn her "Cool As A Cucumber" shirt just yesterday. And yes, it had a cartoon cucumber on it. The cucumber sat on an ice cube with its legs crossed.

"Like I said," Shelby repeated. She was firmer this time. "It's a *developing* storm, and we will *most likely* be fine since we aren't close to the ocean. But Bob and Dotty want to tell you everything themselves. We should all hear the information from one source." This was interesting to me. Bob and Dotty spent most of the time coming up with bizarre daily themes for camp like "Superheroes Day!", "Oopy Gloopy Day!", and "Backwards Day!" I didn't think they could focus on serious things.

"Why aren't we evacuating?" Holly asked. Evacuation. Now *that* sounded scary. It sounded scarier than when we had a fire drill at school because the toaster burned the nurse's grilled cheese and set off all the smoke alarms.

"We probably won't need to evacuate," Shelby answered. She walked to the door. "We are pretty far away from the ocean, so we might just feel the *effects* of the storm." I don't think she wanted to answer any more of our questions. "Ladies, why don't we just head right on down to the Mess Hall for that update from Bob and Dotty? Is everyone ready to roll?" Shelby pumped her fist and stomped her feet in rhythm. *Uh-oh*, I thought, *we're about to march again*.

"Give me your left-left, your left-right-left," Shelby sang. Shelby would sing this tune to get us moving. Sometimes she just shouted, "Give me your left!" and we would all pop up, ready to go. Because of the news Shelby had just shared, we got our lefts and rights moving pretty quickly.

"Shelby! Shelby!" Tara called out as we started walking. "What was the good news?"

"Oh! We're having hot dogs for dinner tonight," Shelby said. Too bad Shelby didn't give us the good news first. Hot dogs were one of my favorite foods. As I thought about squirting ketchup and mustard all over my hot dog, I realized something awful. My parents were in Florida!

Chapter 6

THE SANDPIPER BUNK SURPRISE

Unfortunately, Bob and Dotty's meeting about the storm didn't make me feel much better. I barely tasted my hot dog. But I may have put too much ketchup and mustard on it.

"Noodle, Bob and Dotty will let you know if there's any issue with your parents," Shelby assured me. We were walking back to the cabin. "Since there's nothing you can do, it's best not to worry about the what-ifs." Those were not words my mother lived by. My mom worried about everything. I'm sure my mom was more worried about me than she was about being caught in the middle of a hurricane. I wrote to my parents as soon as we got back to our cabin. I let them know I was okay. That way my mom would have one less thing to worry about if she and Daddy were stuck in a storm.

Friday, July 10

Dear Mom and Dad,

I just came from an all-camp meeting. I hope you are okay. Bob and Dotty told us about Hurricane Hilda. It must be right near you. They sounded very serious. It must be a big deal. Tonight's dinner didn't have any theme at all!

I couldn't really hear Bob and Dotty over Janice and Marla. They kept saying, "Oh my goodness!" after everything Bob said. Bob talked a lot about how they had been in plenty of emergency situations before. He said we'll ride out the storm. I don't think they would say, "we're completely panicking!" right? How are they going to deliver food if the roads get flooded? At least we'll always have bug juice. That stuff can probably survive anything. Especially the orange flavor.

I want you to know that I'm okay. You don't have to worry about me. I will probably never love camp like Jill. But between the different sports and preparing for my next time on Radio Hillside, I guess I will manage for the next—and LAST—two weeks of camp.

I hope you get this letter in time and the envelope doesn't get soaked. Too bad we didn't get waterproof paper.

Sealed with showers—the rain kind. The camp showers are gross and filled with cobwebs.

Your daughter, Noodle

I started to write more over the next couple of days. Maybe I was inspired by the drama surrounding an impending storm. I jotted down an outline for a story called "The Sandpiper Storm Chasers." I made each of my bunkmates into a character. I called my character "Lauren" to disguise my identity. I had always wanted to write stories in my journal. But during the first few days at Camp Hillside, I mostly wrote down my thoughts on camp. And my ideas for the Noodle Newman Radio Show.

Tara went to check the clothesline outside and came back with her dry swimsuit. A gust of wind blew into the room when she opened the door. I swatted away any mosquitos with my journal. I waved my journal a little too strongly. Some pages flew out. Aries caught one in mid-air as she climbed up to her bunk.

"Give it back! I mean, *please* give it back," I said. I grabbed at the page in Aries' hand. She avoided me without losing her place.

"Wait a second, Noodle," Aries said, waving me off. "Let me finish this."

"Please, Aries," I pleaded. I quickly gathered the papers that had fallen on the floor. Aries jumped up to her bunk and continued reading.

"Listen to this, you guys," Aries said. She started to read out loud. She ignored me completely. "Friendship bracelets: are people still your friends after the bracelet starts to smell and you have to cut it off?" As she read, the other girls in the bunk stopped what they were doing. They listened intently.

"What are you reading, Aries?" Buffy asked. She came closer so she didn't miss anything. Aries shuffled through a few more papers.

"Ooh, this looks like a story. It's called 'The Sandpiper Bunk Surprise.' The main character is named Lauren . . ." Aries paused for a moment. Then she read my story out loud. I held my breath. Why couldn't Aries just give me back my papers? Everyone stopped and listened as she continued to read. They actually laughed when they were supposed to. When Aries finished reading, a few of the girls actually clapped. For me!

"Noodle, you're such a good writer," Charlie said. "You're like a comedian. Why have you kept this stuff from us?" The other girls agreed.

"Honestly, Noodle. This is pretty good," Aries added. "You should do something with it. You can use your writing as material for Radio Hillside!"

"Oh . . . uh . . . sure," I said. I didn't sound that excited out loud. But inside, I knew I would love that.

Shelby came back inside the cabin from her nightly check on the garbage bins. "Shelby, when do we go back to Radio Hillside?" Aries asked. "Noodle's been writing some great material."

Shelby looked surprised. Then she smiled happily. "I think we're on again this Monday. I'll double check for you. While you wait, put together your best ideas. You're going first, remember?" Shelby asked with an encouraging nod.

"I will," I answered. I nodded back. It felt like the sun shone straight down on me. It didn't really, though. It was another rainy day. I didn't even get upset when Holly made the choking gesture again. She immediately let go of her neck at the first loud crack of thunder.

"The hurricane is here!" Buffy shrieked. She grabbed Charlie's arm. Charlie also shrieked, but only because Buffy squeezed her so hard. Marla looked out the window nervously. Maybe she thought a giant hurricane would whirl by our cabin at any moment. She ran over to Shelby.

"Shelby, can I call my parents?" Marla asked. "They can pick me up before the hurricane comes."

"Marla, no!" Shelby responded. "You heard Bob and Dotty. We're just in for some stormy weather. We won't experience the full power of a hurricane. Come on, now! You can handle a little rain!"

"Rain, rain go away, come again another day," Holly sang. Tara joined in. She tried to harmonize with Holly. She was unsuccessful. Buffy rolled her eyes and put her hands over her ears. Charlie covered her head with a pillow.

"Let's play some card games until it's time for bed. What are we going to play? Hearts? Crazy Eights? Rummy?" Shelby would have gone through the entire history of card games if her walkie-talkie hadn't stopped her.

"Shelby, this is Base. Do you read me?" a crackly voice said.

"Go for Shelby. I read you, Base." Shelby quickly handed the cards to Aries. Aries shuffled them like she was a professional. Nobody picked up their cards. We all sat frozen and listened to Shelby and the walkie-talkie.

"Shelby, we need you to check the Goldfinch, Cardinal, and Chickadee garbage areas tonight. Coverage is stretched thin with the approaching storm."

"Roger that," Shelby answered. "Ten-four, Base." We all stared at Shelby. We were amazed at her walkie-talkie lingo. Shelby didn't have time for our compliments. She put her boots on with a sigh.

"Girls, pick a card game. Keep yourselves busy before bed," Shelby said. She sounded distracted. "I'll be back as soon as I can. Hopefully I'll only be gone for twenty minutes. Maybe thirty minutes. Just stay inside until I get back." Holly and Tara nodded at each other suspiciously as soon as Shelby left.

"Ladies, it's time for an *unofficial* cabin meeting," Tara said. She motioned us over. She waited until she had our attention. "Tonight, Holly and I have a little 'Sandpiper Adventure' planned."

"It's time to make things more exciting with all this rain," Holly added. "Who's in?" Marla and Janice instantly said yes.

Charlie shrugged. She said, "I'm in, too. I'm tired of losing to you at cards, Aries. No offense."

Holly scanned the room. She stared at Buffy.

"If y'all are doing it, so am I," Buffy said with a shrug. I wished Buffy had been wearing her "Resist 'Pear' Pressure" T-shirt, but she was in her pajamas.

"What if it's a bad idea?" I whispered to Aries. I knew it was. Most of Holly and Tara's pranks failed. Or made a mess. Or both. They made ketchup packet cannons that sprayed everywhere. They tossed pinecones into toilets and made them overflow. That one didn't make the janitors happy.

"Hey, you two chatter-bugs," Tara said. She walked over to Aries and me. She casually flipped her hair back even though she was wearing a headband. "Are you in?"

"We're in," Aries said in a loud and clear voice. "We're in," she whispered again, just to me. I guess I wouldn't be resisting Aries' peer or "pear" pressure tonight.

"So, what are we doing?" Buffy asked.

"Oh, it's going to be good," Tara said. She giggled mischievously.

"It's going to be *epic*," Holly corrected her. She motioned for us to come closer, even though we were already right next to her and Tara's bed.

Chapter 7

NOT-SO-SWEET REVENGE

"Okay! Here's the plan," Holly began when she was certain she had everyone's attention. "We're going to surprise the Goldfinches. We'll sneak up to their windows. Then, we're going to make some ghost noises. We'll scare the living daylights out of them!"

"*That's* your prank?" Charlie asked. She scrunched up her nose. Charlie had started horseback riding lessons this summer with a girl from the Goldfinches' cabin named Nicole. They were good friends. It made perfect sense why Charlie wasn't interested in Holly and Tara's scheme.

"Relax. I'm sure Char-cole will survive some harmless fun," Holly said. She used her sweetest voice. Holly called Charlie and Nicole "Char-cole" when she saw them together. "This is a little prank. It'll be so funny later. You guys can talk about it when you're back in the saddle or whatever it is you horse-people say." Charlie still looked annoyed, but she didn't say anything else.

"But do we have to go out tonight? In this rain?" Marla asked. Now *she* scrunched up her nose.

"Yes! We have to get the Goldfinches back for their water bottle prank," Tara said. "They embarrassed us in front of the whole Mess Hall." This wasn't the best argument. The Mess Hall was one of the busiest, noisiest places at camp. No one really paid much attention to the other cabins.

"C'mon, you guys," Holly urged. "We'll run over there really quick and yell 'BOO!' at the top of our lungs. Then we'll see their reactions. We'll run right back to the cabin after. Shelby won't even know we're gone. If she does, what's the worst she can do?" Tara nodded her head. She acted like they had done this a million times. We all looked at each other. We waited for someone to come up with a good excuse for why we didn't have to do this. And if even we did, we didn't need to in the middle of a storm. Marla was the quickest thinker.

"I'll stay behind in case Shelby comes back and asks questions," she said. She sat on her bed with smug satisfaction.

"Great idea, Marla," Holly nodded. Charlie opened her mouth to say something. Then she must have realized there was no point.

"It doesn't look like the rain's even coming down that hard anymore," Tara said. Then a stream of rain hit the window.

"We need to hurry if we're going to make it back before Shelby does," Holly said. She motioned for Janice and Buffy to get moving. They always took the longest to do anything. Janice put her boots on over her pajamas with a sigh. After Janice caved in, Buffy mumbled, "Okay, fine." She got her boots, too.

"That didn't take much convincing," Charlie muttered. Like a row of dominoes, the rest of us did the same as Janice and Buffy. Aries jumped down from the upper bunk. She was already wearing her poncho. Aries whispered to me, "We're in this together. Let's go." We both pulled on our boots with a grunt.

"Gimme your left!" Holly shouted. She did a bad imitation of Shelby's chant. It made this horrible prank seem even worse. Holly motioned for us to follow her into the soggy and chilly night air. We all moved slowly. I wish we hadn't agreed to Holly and Tara's plan.

"Let's go, let's go," Tara said. Her flashlight swung back and forth like a lighthouse. Holly put her hand on Tara's flashlight and pushed it down.

"Everyone! Keep your flashlights low," Holly snapped as we hurried along the pathway. We headed toward the Goldfinches' cabin. We heard an owl hoot from the not-so-distant woods.

"Being out here in the dark gives me the creeps," Buffy moaned. She grabbed Charlie's arm tightly. We made it across the field in record time. We only had to stop twice. The first time was so Janice could grab her boot that somehow fell off. The second time was when we hid behind a tree because we thought we heard Shelby coming. I nervously fiddled with my glasses as we waited under the cover of a big pine tree. Holly poked her head out, trying to see inside the Goldfinch's cabin. Now this prank definitely felt like a bad idea.

"What if we get caught?" Janice asked. She said out loud exactly what I was thinking. "What if something goes wrong?"

"Nothing's going to go wrong," Holly snapped. "Besides, we're closer to the Goldfinches' cabin than to ours. It's too late to turn back now."

Janice pursed her lips but said nothing.

"Come on, girls! This is what camp is all about," Tara said. She tried too hard to sound cheery. No one whooped or cheered in support.

Instead, Charlie said, "You guys, I'm freezing." She blew on her hands and rubbed them together to show how cold she was. I wished I had worn a warmer sweatshirt under my rain poncho.

"I'm cold, too," Buffy said. Her teeth chattered. I wondered if Buffy was wearing her shirt that said "Cool Girl" with a picture of a popsicle on it. That would've been a fitting choice.

"I can't feel my hands," Janice said. "I think I might have frostbite . . . or maybe hypothermia. You can still get hypothermia in the summer, right?"

"Yes, you can," Aries said immediately. The threat of hypothermia was enough for Charlie.

"I don't want to do this anymore," Charlie said firmly. "Let's go back." We all immediately agreed.

"Okay, fine. You win," Holly said with an angry sigh. She turned quickly. She nearly slipped on a muddy patch. We all followed behind. We were too cold to speak.

"I wish I'd brought gloves to camp," I said after a moment. I was trying to distract myself from feeling the cold.

"I actually *did* bring gloves," Aries said, "Except I left them in the cabin."

"What would you have brought, Charlie?" I asked. I glanced over at her. She always found ways to quietly include me in her conversations. Now seemed like a good time to repay the favor. Holly shot me a look as if to say, "Who do you think you are?" She quickly turned away when she realized that I was actually helping her.

"I would've packed my favorite winter hat. It has a huge white pom-pom," Charlie said. She patted the top of her head.

"Buffy, what would you have brought?" I asked. I'd managed to turn this horrible excursion into a fun game. I silently thanked my mom for all the times she had done this with Jill and me.

"Hmmm . . . I'd pick a scarf," Buffy said. She added, "with *matching* gloves."

"And those thick, wooly socks," Janice chimed in. "That's what I would've brought."

"I would've brought a jet pack so that I could speed back to the cabin," Tara said. She hugged herself tightly. Holly shot Tara an annoyed look.

"I wish I were Marla right about now," Charlie joked. "She's probably complaining about being *too* warm and dry." We all laughed. No one felt bad for Marla.

"Can we stop for a second? I need to clean off my glasses," I said. I used my damp shirt as a cloth. I only smudged my glasses even more. I was about to use another part of my shirt when Holly grabbed my poncho and tugged me up.

"We're almost there," Holly said firmly. She didn't hide the irritation in her voice. "Let's keep moving." When we were about to start walking, Buffy pointed to an animal about twenty feet away.

"Hey, what's that black and white thing over there?" Buffy asked. Everyone looked where she pointed.

"What's a cat doing outside in the rain?" Janice asked. "Here kitty, kitty!" she called. She put out her hand. Aries smacked her hand down.

"That black and white thing is not a cat!" Aries shrieked as the animal started moving in our direction. "It's a skunk!"

"What do we do?" Tara shrieked. She wrapped her poncho around her body. All I knew about skunks was that you had to take a bath in tomato juice if you got sprayed. I hope we wouldn't have to find out if that was true.

"Why don't we go *around* the skunk?" Aries suggested. She pointed toward the woods. "We'll make a big loop and stay out of its way."

"What if there are more?" Janice asked. "Don't skunks travel in packs?"

"I don't think skunks travel in packs. It's not like they're a school of lions," Buffy said. She was trying to be helpful.

"A *family* of lions is actually called a *pride*," Aries said. She was about to launch into a National Geographic special she'd watched.

"You guys, shhh!" Holly hissed. "If you don't pipe down, we're all going to get sprayed!" Holly took Aries' advice of

heading into the woods. She walked toward a small hill in the distance.

"This should be far enough away," Holly said. She pointed to the skunk. It didn't look like it was moving. "We can head to the cabin from here." At that moment, we heard a rustling in the leaves only a few feet from where we were standing. What on earth could it be now?

Chapter 8

A SSSSURPRISE FOR THE SANDPIPERS

"It's a snake!" yelled Tara. She covered her eyes for some reason. I hated snakes too, but I knew that covering my eyes wouldn't make the snake go away.

"Eek! A snake! I hate snakes!" screamed Buffy. Her shriek was even more piercing than Tara's. She was petrified of snakes, bats, and clowns. For some reason, she was okay with spiders.

"It's probably just a chipmunk or a squirrel," Holly said. She quietly picked up her pace. Janice couldn't stay calm anymore. She simply screamed and ran down the hill in a panic. Foolishly, we all followed Janice down the hill. As we neared the bottom, I tripped over a rock and fell down hard. My glasses flew off. They landed in a patch of thick brush.

"I lost my glasses! I can't see!" I shouted. Aries dashed over and circled her flashlight around me. She had barely looked around before Holly pulled her aside.

"I don't think you're going to find Noodle's glasses right now," Holly said. She sounded more annoyed than supportive. Did she know that I could hear every word of their conversation? "We need to get back to the cabin *now*." Oh, so *now* Holly thought we should return to our cabin.

"Wait. I'll leave my sock out here as a marker," Aries said. She slipped off her rain boot. She peeled off her wet sock and placed it on the ground next to me. "I'll go out first thing tomorrow and look again." I would have thanked Aries for being such a good friend if I wasn't so upset about losing my glasses.

"I'll come back with you, Aries. It's too dark to see anything right now," Charlie said. She took one more look around the clearing.

"You can always order a new pair of glasses, Noodle," Tara said after I tripped over a branch. "Or get contacts!"

"But how? I can't just go to my eye doctor. She's at least four hours away!" I cried. Janice shined her flashlight up the hill once more. I think she was trying to be helpful.

"Guys! I think I found Noodle's glasses!" she yelled excitedly. She ran back up the hill. In an instant, Janice tripped on the same rock I had just fallen over. We all heard a loud *thump* as Janice hit the ground.

"Ow!" Janice cried. She clutched her forehead. "My head really hurts."

"She's bleeding!" Charlie said. She rushed over to Janice.

"Oh no, oh no, oh no! Janice is bleeding!" Tara screamed.

"Don't die on us, Janice!" Buffy cried. She hovered over Janice nervously.

"She's not going to die," Aries snapped. She shone her flashlight on Janice. "She's still conscious, so that's a good sign."

"We have to get help! Now!" Charlie said. She sounded slightly hysterical.

"I'll go get Shelby," Holly said. Her voice was shaky. "Everyone, stay here." Holly ran to the cabin. We all clustered around Janice to comfort her. No one cared about the skunk—or my glasses—anymore.

"Janice, let me take a closer look at that cut," Aries said. She wedged the flashlight in her armpit and carefully turned Janice's head toward her.

"Oww!" Janice cried as Aries plucked a leaf from her forehead.

"That big, dark leaf made your cut look like a huge gash. It's actually just a small cut," Aries said proudly. "You're definitely going to live." We waited for Shelby for a long time. We huddled together under a tree in silence. It would have been a great bonding moment if we weren't so scared and cold.

I focused on my chattering teeth as I went through a list of all the things I couldn't do without my glasses. *I can't play soccer. I can't do archery. That would be way too dangerous. I can probably practice piano. Wait. I'm at camp! I don't have to practice piano. Ugh! I can't read. Can I write? I could probably write if I kept my head really close to the paper. How will I do the radio show? Can I memorize my script? What if we do the show tomorrow? What if that's my last ch—* My internal monologue would've continued if Aries hadn't jumped up and yelled "Shelby! Over here!"

"What in the blazes is going on?" Shelby demanded. Shelby was really mad. When she saw Janice quietly clutching her head, Shelby's anger softened. "Janice, oh goodness, are you alright?"

"I'm okay," Janice said. "My head is throbbing a bit. It's not too bad." Shelby gently turned Janice's head to inspect the wound.

"It's only a minor cut," Aries said with authority. I imagined Aries holding an imaginary medical chart with all of Janice's vital signs.

"But there's a big bump," Janice added. She was clearly in need of sympathy.

"Let's get you back to the bunk," Shelby said. She gently helped Janice to her feet. "I have an ice pack in our first aid kit." Janice was a little unsteady at first. She may have been acting dramatic. After a moment, she appeared perfectly fine. We were about to head back to the bunk when Shelby spied me clutching Charlie's arm tightly.

"Noodle, where are your glasses?" Shelby asked. I could tell she was looking right at me.

"I'm sorry, what?" I asked, stalling for time.

"Your glasses, Noodle," Shelby repeated, more urgently. "Where are they?" Shelby knew I always wore my glasses.

"They're . . . uh . . . they're um . . . well, you see," I tried to find something to say.

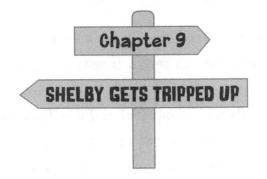

"Noodle lost her glasses earlier," Holly said. "So we all went looking for them. That's why we were out just now."

"Uh . . . yup," I added after a moment's pause. "That's what happened." I had waited a moment too long.

"Really?" Shelby asked. She raised her eyebrows. "You were wearing your glasses at dinner, though. And we didn't walk back to the cabin this way . . ."

"I, uh . . . I . . ." I didn't know what to say.

"Noodle lost them tonight. *After* dinner. We went out for a quick walk," Holly said. She tried not to get trapped in her lie. "We thought we'd save you the trouble by looking for her glasses ourselves." It was obvious that Shelby didn't believe Holly, but no one wanted to add onto Holly's already shaky story.

"It'll be nearly impossible to find the glasses once we leave this spot," Shelby said. She shook her head.

"I was going to go back and look for Noodle's glasses tomorrow morning," Aries said. She gestured to the area where she had put down her sock. Shelby squinted toward where Aries had pointed. Then she sighed.

"Charlie, can you get that ice pack for Janice back in the cabin? You just have to smash it against something hard. Then have Janice put it on her head," Shelby said. "Aries, show me exactly where your sock is. *I'll* go look for Noodle's glasses." Shelby's voice was weary. "Everyone else, go back to the cabin. Now! And don't move an inch until I get there. I'll be back as soon as I can. Who knows when that will be . . ."

Aries led Shelby off. The rest of the us hurried back to the cabin. Charlie supported Janice, who easily could have walked on her own. Buffy held me by the elbow and told me which steps to avoid. She was a half-second too late just about every time. When we finally got back to our bunk, Marla sat up sharply and rubbed her eyes.

"Marla, were you asleep?" Holly asked.

"What? No. I wasn't asleep," Marla said with a yawn.

"I can't believe you fell asleep!" Holly said. She shook her head in disapproval. "You were supposed to cover for us in case Shelby came back. And by cover, I didn't mean 'cover' your head and fall asleep!"

"Our lookout was only *looking* at her pillow!" Tara added. She copied Holly's annoyed tone as best she could. Some of the other girls murmured in agreement. I was too busy looking for dry pajamas to pay attention.

"Sorry! I didn't realize how tired I was," Marla said sheepishly. "It was a long day." After a pause, Marla asked, "Hey Janice, what happened to you?"

"I fell. It's really slippery outside," Janice explained. Charlie handed her the ice pack.

"And where are Shelby and Aries?" Marla asked. Her questions made us replay the night's events.

"They're looking for my glasses," I said. I squinted in Marla's general direction.

"Your glasses? What happened to your glasses?" Marla asked. Holly butted in to retell the story. She left out the part about all this being her fault.

As we changed out of our damp clothes and got ready for bed a second time, Aries burst back into the cabin. She was soaking wet.

"You guys, now *Shelby's* hurt!" Aries cried. She pointed toward the area of the woods we'd just come from. "A big tree branch fell on her! She got knocked over. Then *she* slipped on some rocks! She hurt her leg. I think it's really bad." Aries blurry face looked even paler than normal. Shelby's injury must have been serious.

"We need to call somebody!" shrieked Tara. She looked for a phone. It was the worst time for a camp to have a no-technology rule. Shelby's walkie-talkie was the only way we could contact anyone, and Shelby had it. Before we could figure out what to do, we heard a golf cart whiz by. Aries poked her head out the door and saw that it was heading in Shelby's direction.

"Wait for me! I'm coming for you, Shelby!" Aries wailed into the darkness as she ran after the golf cart.

Chapter 10

A RUDE INTRODUCTION

We all sat around the cabin. We felt terrible. Buffy and Janice said every prayer they had learned at Sunday school. We all hoped that everything would be okay. I was quiet. I was sorry for everything that had gone wrong. The cabin door swung open before I blamed myself for not bringing an extra pair of glasses. A blast of wind blew in. It made my bedsheets flutter. Aries slunk inside first. Dotty followed her. There was another tall girl with them. I didn't recognize her. I couldn't recognize anything without my glasses.

"Good evening, ladies," Dotty said. Her normally sweet voice sounded a bit tired. "Actually, it's not such a good evening. Shelby's a bit banged up. She will spend the night in the Health Center after she returns from the Emergency Room." We all gasped at the news.

"Will she be alright?" Tara asked. She spoke in a quiet voice. That was unusual for Tara. "I feel just awful that she got hurt. It's just so—" I was certain that Holly had shot Tara a look and warned her not to talk anymore. Tara immediately shut up.

"We're hoping Shelby will be okay. She was in quite a bit of pain, but still in good spirits. That's Shelby for you," Dotty answered. She sighed and shook her head. "Before Shelby left, she asked me to give these to you, Noodle." Dotty fished around for something in her pocket and put down a jumble of crooked plastic on my trunk.

"Yeesh," Aries muttered under her breath.

"You're going to need some tape until we can get you a new pair," Dotty said. She pointed to the remains of my glasses. I tried to put them on. They were too bent up to even fit over my ears.

"At least the lenses aren't broken," I said with a shrug. *I could still do Radio Hillside with these things*, I thought. Dotty cleared her throat loudly.

"Ladies, I want to introduce you to Tabitha," Dotty said. She pointed to the stranger who stood silently behind her. "Tabitha will be your counselor for now." Tabitha wore saggy, ripped jeans. Her choppy haircut was streaked with purple. She stepped forward.

"Hey," she said with a quick nod. She gave a half smile that sort of looked like a smirk. Tabitha shifted her weight. She looked uncomfortable to be there. We all quietly said our "hi's" and "hellos."

Dotty leaned over and whispered in Tabitha's ear. Tabitha stood up straighter.

"And I, uh, I wanted to say that it's, uh, so nice to meet all of you," Tabitha said with forced excitement. We just stared at her. Nobody knew what to make of Tabitha.

"Girls, while she is your new counselor, Tabitha also happens to be my niece. I know she'll take good care of you

for however long we need her to," Dotty said. She waited for Tabitha to nod. She did, after a moment.

"I'll leave you all to get some rest now that you have met. It's been a long night for all of us," Dotty added. "I'm sure Tabitha will take good care of all of you." Dotty quickly adjusted her bright yellow rain hat and patted Bob on the arm. He hadn't said a word the whole time. She glanced at Tabitha and then hurried Bob out of the cabin. Tabitha eyed us cautiously as soon as Bob and Dotty were gone.

"It's late, so here's the deal," Tabitha began. She flipped her hair. "I've been to camp before. I practically grew up here. I know *all* the tricks. Let's make things easy: I don't bother you, and you don't bother me. If we can do that, we'll get along just fine." We all must have looked pretty shocked because Tabitha slightly softened her tone. "Don't get me wrong. I'll do the basic things that I'm supposed to do. I'll make sure you stay alive, blah, blah, blah . . . "

"Oh. My. Goodness," Buffy whispered. If Buffy's mouth had stayed open any longer, a mosquito might have flown in.

"And one last thing," Tabitha said. She had her hand on the door. "That baloney prank you tried to pull tonight . . . that won't fly with me. You girls are a bunch of amateurs. You didn't even cover your tracks for cripe's sake!" She mumbled that she'd "see us at whenever o'clock" and disappeared into the night. We all sat around. We were completely speechless after Tabitha left. Marla was the first to break the silence.

"If we're being honest, Shelby was a little too 'yippee, everything-is-awesome' for my taste," Marla said. She pretended to shake a pom-pom like a cheerleader. "But compared to Tabitha, I'll take 'everything is awesome.'"

"Me too," Buffy agreed. "Tabitha looks like she eats lemons for breakfast, lunch, and dinner."

"Or maybe rotten bug juice," Janice said. She laid back down on her pillow. She slowly placed the ice pack back on her head.

"How is she related to Bob and Dotty?" I asked. "It doesn't seem possible that anyone on their family tree could be so grumpy."

"Who knows? Maybe she's not so bad," Charlie offered. No one nodded in agreement.

"Were you guys even listening?" Holly asked. "Tabitha basically just gave us the freedom to do whatever we want!" Tara mustered a supportive smile. No one else felt like celebrating.

"I just hope Shelby comes back soon," I said. I fiddled with my broken glasses. Maybe they would somehow bend back to normal.

Chapter 11

BREAKING NEWS

Aries offered to fix my glasses the next morning. She crawled down from her bunk and sat on my bed. I handed her the mess of plastic and lenses. I had wondered about all the camps Aries had been to. Now seemed like a pretty good time to ask her about them.

"So," I started. "You've been to a lot of summer camps, huh?"

"Yep," Aries said without looking up from her work.

"Do you just really like summer camps?" I asked. I laughed a little to try and lighten the mood. Too bad my fake laugh ended up sounding more like a sheep saying "baaaa." Aries looked up briefly but didn't respond. She probably didn't want to talk about it. But I was too curious. I couldn't help myself. "What's your story then?" I had counted to eleven before Aries finally spoke.

"I think my dad likes it better when I'm not in the house," Aries said quietly. "I can't bother him and my stepmom if I'm gone all summer."

"Oh," I said. *I should've kept my big mouth shut!* "I'm sorry, I didn't mean to—"

"I mean, my dad works basically all the time," Aries continued. She didn't seem to hear me. "And my stepmom . . . she's an artist. Well, she *wants* to be. She likes painting more than being a mom. Between you and me," Aries said with a scoff, "I don't think she's great at either." She finally looked up at me. "I don't hate summer camp. But I do kind of hate the fact that my dad and stepmom see them as a place to leave me for two months so they can live their lives."

"Well . . ." I said hesitantly. "I, for one, am glad you came to Camp Hillside. I'm happy to be your friend, Aries De Falco." I reached around her shoulders with one arm and gave her a side-hug. As I did, my elbow knocked into the side of the bunk bed.

"Ouch," I said, pulling my arm back suddenly. "That's totally going to be a huge black and blue mark." Aries nodded her head as I rubbed my elbow.

"Thanks, Noodle. I'm glad I met you, too," Aries said with a small smile. She patted my leg and handed me my glasses. I looked at the frames which were now back in one piece.

"These look pretty good," I said, putting my glasses back on. "Thank you so much, Aries!"

Aries pretended to bow and said, "You're most welcome."

Now that I could sort of see again, I suggested that we go visit Shelby in the Health Center. We arrived at the Health Center and found Shelby lying in bed, her leg propped up on a stack of pillows. She sleepily opened one eye when she heard us come in.

"I am so so so so sorry for what happened," I said. I ignored the fact that Shelby was probably exhausted. "I have never, ever felt worse about anything in my entire life." I hoped Shelby heard the guilt and regret in my voice. I couldn't help but stare at Shelby's leg as I talked. A bright white cast stretched all the way up to her thigh. It looked really painful. And itchy. "I will come and visit you every day until you're better," I promised. It seemed like the right thing to do to make amends for the way things turned out.

"That's very sweet of you, Noodle," Shelby answered. She was now fully awake. "But I'm afraid I won't be staying in here for much longer. I went to the Emergency Room last night and it turns out my leg has a pretty bad break. I wanted to tell all the 'Pipers at once . . . but you should know that I'm leaving camp this afternoon. Bob and Dotty wanted me to head home as soon as possible because of the hurricane that's coming."

"No! You can't leave!" Aries cried. A nearby nurse looked at Aries sharply and hissed, "Shhh!" Aries glared back at her.

"But you're our counselor! How could you leave?" I asked. *How on earth could Shelby leave us with* Tabitha?

"I'm totally bummed out too," Shelby said. She sighed heavily. It felt awful to see Shelby like this. "The doctor said I can't walk on my leg for at least six weeks. And I might need surgery. Plus, with all the hills here . . . I'm afraid I won't be of much use to anybody."

"But even when you're injured, you're so much better than Tabitha," I said.

"A rock would be better," Aries added. "Or a raindrop. Even a puddle." Shelby smiled weakly. Her eyes slowly closed. Aries and I looked at each other. We weren't sure what to do. We were about to get up and leave, but we heard two distinct pairs of footsteps approaching Shelby's bed.

"Good morning, ladies!" a booming voice said. I didn't have to turn around to know it was Bob. Shelby stirred, but she didn't sit up.

"How's the patient?" Dotty asked softly. She smoothed Shelby's hair just like my mom does to me when I was sick.

"I'm doing okay," Shelby said. She tried hard to keep her eyes open.

"You'll be back to tip-top shape in no time, my dear," Dotty said. She smiled warmly.

"Speaking of shapes," Bob said. He eyed my patched-up glasses. "We got in touch with your parents. They called your neighbor, Mrs. Pearson. She'll be overnighting an old pair of your glasses up here. If we're lucky, you'll get them by tomorrow. Let's hope the weather and the mail cooperate with us." I nodded in agreement. Aries had put so much tape on my glasses that they kept sliding down my nose.

"Ladies, we should let Shelby get her rest," Dotty said. She gently guided us out of the Health Center. "I'm sure she'll stop by the cabin before . . . she heads home." Dotty's tone was sad.

"See you later, Shelby," I whispered as Aries and I headed back out into the rain. When we were a safe distance away, Aries and I spoke at the same time.

"I can't believe Shelby's leaving!" I exclaimed, while Aries said, "I can't believe she didn't tell Bob and Dotty that we snuck out in the middle of the storm!" Leave it to Aries to focus on the wrong detail.

"Aries, her leg is broken. She's going home because of that stupid prank," I said firmly.

"Yeah, but imagine how much trouble *we* would be in if Bob and Dotty knew what really happened?" Aries asked. "I wonder what Shelby said . . ."

I was too upset about Shelby to think about how she might have covered for us. Aries and I walked over to the Great Lake where we caught up with the rest of our cabin. We were just in time for candle making. I was glad to have a distraction.

Later, I jotted down an idea I had for a new story. I wanted to call it *The Sandpipers vs. The Skunk*—it's a real stinker. I also needed to write my parents a letter. It had been a long day, particularly with the news about Shelby leaving.

Sunday, July 12

Dear Mom and Dad,

I thought you were supposed to be back from Florida by now. Maybe I forgot when you were coming home. Anyway, I heard that Mrs. Pearson will send my glasses. Thank goodness! I don't know if Bob and Dotty told you, but Shelby got hurt while rescuing my glasses. The story is too long to write.

Trust me when I tell you it was <u>not</u> for a good reason. We had such a hard time saying goodbye to Shelby this afternoon when she came to our cabin. I think Shelby may have cried the most when she came over to me, though I would never tell any of the other girls that.

It stinks that Shelby is leaving. I was just getting used to things around here! I still haven't gotten used to the food. Thank goodness they serve bagels all day.

The rain and wind are worse. That must mean that the storm is coming closer. I hope Great Falls wasn't in the path of the storm. I wish you could tell me what kind of weather we can expect—

A huge crackle of lightning made me look up from my writing. I heard a loud thunderclap. The lights flickered for a moment. Then everything went pitch black.

Chapter 12

SPECIAL DELIVERY

"Did we just lose power?" Buffy asked.

"It looks like the power is out for the whole camp," Aries said. She peered out the window. She dug around in her trunk and found a flashlight. It was so bright that it lit up our entire side of the cabin.

"Where's Tabitha?" Marla asked. I had forgotten all about Tabitha. She was never around. Even though she had made a horrible first impression, she was still technically in charge of us.

"Let's go over to the Goldfinches' cabin and investigate," Holly said. She stood and motioned for everyone to follow her.

"No way," Janice said. She firmly shook her head no. "Not after last time." Holly looked mildly annoyed. She glared at Janice.

"Okay. Well, what if we just went out on the front porch?" Holly asked. Another crackle of thunder followed. A few of the girls screamed.

"I think we should just wait *inside* for Tabitha," Charlie said. We all agreed. We quickly outnumbered Holly. We waited and waited for Tabitha to arrive. We missed our Afternoon Rec period. I skipped archery, which I was secretly happy about. Shower Hour came and went. After all that time on our own, we had run out of card games to play, hair to braid, and dances to choreograph. When dinnertime came, we started to get worried. And hungry.

"Should we just go to the Mess Hall without Tabitha?" Buffy asked. "I'm starving." Then we all heard a loud knock at the door. We were so startled that none of us moved.

"That better not be a bear," Buffy said. She pulled a blanket over her head.

"Since when do bears knock?" Holly snapped. I noticed she hadn't moved to answer the door. Whoever or whatever was outside must have heard us talking and knocked again. They knocked louder this time. Aries leapt down from her bed with a grumble and opened the door. As she did, a huge gust of wind caused the door to fly open and slam against the wall. To our surprise, we saw Kurt. He still looked handsome despite being covered head to toe in soggy rain gear. Kurt held a big box covered with a tarp.

"Hiiii Kuuuurrt," Holly and Tara said together. The other girls were really excited to greet Kurt, too.

"Hello, ladies," Kurt said. He was still charming even when he was rained on. "I've brought you all some food. I'm sure you've heard that we're in 'stay-put' mode for tonight."

"What do you mean, 'stay-put'—" Charlie began to ask.

"—Hey, 'Pipers," Tabitha said as she appeared out of nowhere. "Here I am. Lots of things to prepare with us being on hurricane lockdown and all." Kurt eyed Tabitha suspiciously. He didn't say a word. Tabitha's eyes locked on Kurt. She smiled broadly as he handed her a note.

"Here are some instructions from Bob and Dotty," Kurt told her. She quickly slipped the note into her pocket.

"Cool," Tabitha said with more enthusiasm than we'd ever heard from her.

"Alright then. I've got some more food deliveries to make," Kurt said after a pause. "Hopefully, the storm will head out to sea and the power will be back soon."

"I hope so, too. Hurricanes are the worst!" Tabitha said. She still spoke in a strange, overly friendly voice. "But no hurricane can stop us from having fun! Right, girls?" No one answered her. She gave Kurt one final wave and closed the door. When she was sure he was gone, Tabitha's entire body relaxed into her natural slouch. The real Tabitha had returned. "Well, it looks like it'll be an early night for you girls," Tabitha said dryly.

"What?" Buffy shrieked. "You're joking, right?" Buffy was wearing a purple shirt that said, "I Found This Humerus." There was a picture of a big bone on the front.

"Wait a second. Let's go back to this lockdown—I mean, 'stay put' thing," Aries said. "What exactly does that mean?"

"It means what it says. You don't go anywhere tonight," Tabitha said with a shrug. "It's not like you had big plans, right?"

"It would have been nice to find that information out from you, our counselor. You know, the person who's *responsible* for us?" Aries asked. She looked ready to throttle Tabitha. Tabitha simply shrugged.

"Is anybody hungry?" Tabitha asked. She ignored Aries and acted like nothing had happened. Our stomachs growled. They betrayed our annoyance at Tabitha as she tore open the box of food. We all clustered around her. We were excited to see what might be inside.

"Lunch for dinner?" Marla complained. Inside the box we saw stacks of sandwiches, chips, apples, and cookies. There were also with several bottles of water.

"Marla, be a team player for once," Tabitha said. "There's no 'I' in storm, right?" That sounded just like something her Aunt Dotty might say.

"But there is an 'I' in hurricane," Aries snapped. Tabitha just shot her a look and continued to empty the box.

"Wait. There's no bug juice in here?" Charlie joked. She was trying to lighten the mood. "I can't eat this."

"No caviar?" Tara joined in. She spoke in a fake British accent. "I refuse to eat this rubbish." Her accent wasn't very good, but it made everyone laugh.

"I just wish I hadn't already eaten a sandwich for lunch, that's all," Marla grumbled. She was still annoyed with the meal.

"Yay, turkey!" Janice exclaimed. She grabbed one of the sandwiches. She was the only person actually excited about the food.

"I'm just glad that we don't have to go down to the Mess Hall in this awful weather," Buffy said. It was hard to ignore the racket of rain hitting the cabin.

"It must be a real mess in the Mess Hall," I joked. Everyone laughed. We grew quiet. We were comforted by the food and the rhythm of the rain. We played a few more rounds of cards after lunch-for-dinner. I read some of my stories for our evening entertainment. Tabitha pretended like she wasn't paying attention. I could tell she was listening to every word. After a while, it got too dark to see.

"Well, I guess it's time for bed," Tabitha announced. She looked at her watch and pretended to yawn.

"But it's only eight-thirty!" Aries complained.

"Well, we should really be conserving our flashlights," Tabitha said with a shrug. Since Tabitha was the only one who seemed to have access to the news, we had no choice but to agree with her.

"This weather is so noisy!" Buffy complained after we climbed into bed. She was right. The sound of the pouring rain mixed with the near-constant thunder made it hard to sleep.

"I hate this storm. It's horrible!" Marla cried. She clamped a pillow over her head. Little did we know that the storm's real horrors were yet to come.

Chapter 13

THE WET WAKE UP CALL

The steady *drip-drip-drip* of the rain hitting the roof wasn't more calming on the second night of the hurricane. We all did our best to ignore the whistling wind and the crackling trees. I lay in bed half-asleep and imagined my amazing return to Radio Hillside. *But without power, no one will be going on the radio,* my inner voice reminded me. *Shhh!* I told myself. I tried to hold onto the fantasy. When I drifted off to sleep, I was well on my way to becoming an international superstar. It must have been around midnight when Tara let out a shriek from her bunk.

"What's going on?" Buffy mumbled from the next bunk over.

"My bed!" Tara screamed. I saw her shadowy figure leap onto Marla's bunk. "It's soaked!"

"Did you, um, have an accident?" Holly asked. She was still groggy.

"No! Of course not!" Tara cried. "My comforter and my sheets are all wet . . . it's from the wall or something." Holly climbed up to investigate.

"Hmm, it *is* all wet," Holly confirmed. She patted around Tara's bed.

"We need some light," Aries said. She quickly flicked on her flashlight. It didn't take much light to reveal that the wall was puffed out in a very weird way. "That doesn't look good. I think there's a leak."

"I'm not taking any chances with *my* stuff," Holly said. She bundled up her bedding and moved it over to Marla and Charlie's bunk.

"Come on, Tara. Let's get *your* wet things away from the wall," Charlie said. She shot Holly a sideways glance of disapproval as she helped Tara strip her bed.

"Um, guys . . . where's Tabitha?" I asked. I searched for her darkened presence. We all gasped. We were alone in the middle of a hurricane. With no supervision and no way to contact the rest of the camp. For a second time.

"We've been abandoned!" Buffy shrieked. Her eyes widened with fear. Aries poked her head out the door and looked around.

"Tabitha? Tabitha, are you out there?" she called into the night. The only answer that came back was the sound of the howling wind and rain.

"Oh no, oh no, oh no," Marla whimpered. "I knew I should have had my parents come get me. I should have *insisted* that I call home . . . I should have packed up my bags and . . ." I surprised even myself by speaking.

"You guys, we've got to stay calm. We can't panic," I said. I tried to appear composed even though I wore a ridiculous pair of crooked, taped-up glasses.

"Noodle's right," Aries agreed. "If we panic, we can't think. We need a plan." We all looked back and forth at each other, waiting for someone to come up with the solution. Again, I found myself speaking first.

"Why don't Aries and I go to the Goldfinches' cabin and get help?" I suggested. "And we won't try to scare anyone this time," I added before Holly could get any grand ideas.

"But if Bob and Dotty find out that Tabitha wasn't around, we'll lose our freedom," Holly said. "We get to come and go as we please. No other cabin gets to do that."

"That wall doesn't look it's going to hold," Aries said. She pointed to a trickle of water that dribbled from the bottom of the bulge.

"We can just deal with things in the morning. I'm sure nothing's going to happen to us tonight," Holly said. She confidently folded her arms across her chest. "Tara, you can just . . . uh . . . sleep on the rug."

"Sleep on the rug?" Tara exclaimed. "You want me to sleep on that dirty old thing?"

"I thought it might be more comfortable than sharing my tiny mattress," Holly said. "But fine, you and I can sleep in opposite directions."

Holly tugged at her mattress, but it didn't move. She tried again and pulled much harder. This time, instead of just moving the mattress, Holly dragged the entire bunk bed. The bed ran right into the giant bulge in the wall. All the water gushed out in an instant. It made an enormous puddle on the floor.

"Save yourselves!" Marla screamed. She started to run toward the door. She plowed right into me and knocked me into the corner of my trunk. Even though I would probably have a bruise, the pain from my fall brought me back to my senses.

"Aries, come on! You and I will go for help," I said. I grabbed Aries. She was still hypnotized by the puddle. "Everyone else, move your stuff to the other side of the room!" I have no idea what came over me. I knew Shelby would have been proud. "Aries, come on! Move it!"

Chapter 14

HOTEL HILLSIDE

Aries and I threw on our rain gear and hurried out into the night. Neither of us said much as we sprinted across the field to the Goldfinches' cabin. I hoped Shelby had been friendly to their counselor, Pam, so that she'd be willing to help us. Shelby was friendly to everyone, though, so who was I kidding?

When we got to their cabin, Aries and I banged on their door. We were still huffing and puffing. Instead of opening the door, the Goldfinches merely screamed at the sound of our knocking.

"It's a ghost!" some girl screeched.

"Wait, no! It looks like Noodle, and another girl in their bunk . . . Arlene, I think." That must've been Charlie's friend, Nicole. Thank goodness!

"It's *Aries*," Aries said with a hiss. Pam opened the door a moment later.

"Girls, what's going on?" Pam asked. She looked thoroughly alarmed. "What on earth are you doing out of your cabin in the middle of the storm?"

"We have a problem. A big problem," I began.

"There's a leak in our cabin and we can't find Tabitha," Aries said. She looked longingly at the Goldfinches' dry, puddle-free room. "We couldn't call for help, so we came to you."

"Oh, you poor things!" Pam said. She wiped away a trickle of rain that ran down my cheek. "Goldfinches, you sit tight. I'm going to help our neighbors. I'll be back as soon as I can." Pam threw on her poncho and hopped into her rain boots as she hustled us out the door.

"Thanks for helping us, Pam," I said. I was grateful to have a grown-up around, even if Pam was only about nineteen years old.

"I'm guessing Tabitha was . . . unavailable?" Pam asked as we hurried back to our cabin. "Interesting." Maybe Pam and Tabitha were friends. It didn't seem possible that Tabitha had any friends, though.

We burst into the cabin and pushed the door shut. Even though we had only been gone for about fifteen minutes, the room was a mess.

"What in the . . ." Pam said. Her voice trailed off as she moved her flashlight around the cabin. Everyone's trunks and bunk beds had been pushed to the far side of the room. The girls were all huddled together on Charlie and Janice's bunk. They had turned the bed into a fortress of mattresses. Tabitha came bursting through the door before Pam could respond.

"What the heck is going on in here?" Tabitha yelled. Her tone softened when she saw Pam. "Oh, Pam! Hey. What are you doing here?"

"Well, Noodle and Aries came over to my cabin because—" Pam began.

"You know what, Pam? We should take this conversation outside," Tabitha said sweetly. She guided Pam out of the cabin. They spoke quietly. They were too quiet for us to hear! In less than five minutes, Tabitha somehow sent Pam on her way without another word and also radioed down to base.

"Well, Sandpipers. It looks like you're going to move into Camp Hillside's finest motel," Tabitha said. She clipped the walkie-talkie to her pants.

"They're bringing us to town? To stay at the Great Bear Lodge?" Marla asked. An eager smile spread across her face. "I love the pancakes they serve at breakfast!"

"No, silly. You're being relocated to the basement of the Rec Center," Tabitha said like that was the obvious answer. "They're setting up cots for you now."

"But what about all our stuff?" Buffy asked. "I've got to have my things. What if I need something . . . like my nose spray? I get congested very easily, you know."

"Relax," Tabitha said. She rolled her eyes. "Just pack what you need. And bring some tissues or something." Aries wasn't taking any chances. She began stuffing as much as she could into her backpack. That seemed like a smart thing to do. I started doing the same thing. I grabbed my "essentials": a water bottle, pens, notebook, and a deck of cards. I didn't want to get bored.

We heard the squeal of brakes outside the cabin a few minutes later. Dotty jumped out of a small van. She held a lantern in her hand. Bob followed close behind. He looked even more rumpled than normal.

"Oh, dear," Dotty said. She shook her head as she took in the chaos of our cabin.

"Maybe this won't look so bad in the daylight," Bob said. He rubbed his eyes sleepily. He didn't sound hopeful as he looked at the damage. "What a time to be without power."

"Ladies, we have had far too much excitement in the Sandpiper cabin lately," Dotty said. She turned her attention to *us* instead of Tabitha. "Let's get you all down to the Rec Center. We're setting up a temporary space for you as we speak."

"But what about our stuff?" Buffy repeated.

"Grab a change of clothes and your rain gear," Dotty advised. She pointed to our coat rack. She must have known that "essential" could be different for each of us.

"But what about all my pictures and decorations?" Marla asked.

"Just take what you absolutely *need*, Marla. Don't take what you *want*," Dotty said. Her voice was a little firmer. "Now, let's put on our boots and ponchos so that we can get you to the Rec Center. Goodness knows how late it is."

We couldn't stop giggling as we rode in the van down to the Rec Center. Maybe we realized how crazy everything was. Maybe we were super tired. Either way, we had finally started to come together as a cabin. We sang "On Top of Spaghetti" at the top of our lungs. On the second or third time we repeated, "I lost my poor meatball, when somebody sneezed!" Dotty shouted, "Enough!"

That shut us up for a moment. Then we all looked at each other and started laughing again. We were even louder this time.

Before we could start another song, Bob grumbled, "We're here. Grab your things." The rest of the night was a blur. We were so exhausted that we probably would have slept anywhere . . . just not on our wet beds.

Chapter 15

FOREST FOOD FIGHT

The next morning was weird. We woke up with no Shelby, no power, and no cabin. Thank goodness I had some extra stationary tucked away in my journal. It was one of my essential items.

Wednesday, July 15

Dear Mom and Dad,

I'm writing to you from the basement of the Rec Center. Our cabin sprang a leak in the middle of the night. Now we don't have power or a cabin! I can't wait for this hurricane to be over. I used to love having cold cereal at every meal. But I would do anything for a scrambled egg right now.

We've been on the Rainy Day Schedule for too long. Our entertainment options are pretty limited. We can't have movie marathons. I have played every single board game in here. I don't think I can ever pick up a pair of dice again.

The good news is that Bob and Dotty think the power will come back later today or tomorrow. I hope we can do the radio show one more time before this session of camp ends. Who knew that I wouldn't want to come home just so I could be on the radio again?

Until then, here's a soggy sign off from me.

Love, Noodle

"Mail call," Tabitha grunted. She dropped a box on my cot just as I finished my letter. The box bounced off the cot and nearly fell on the floor. I caught it right before it hit the ground. "You must have gotten something important," Tabitha said. "Aunt Dotty told me I had to drop everything and bring this package to you." I was about to say, "Thank you," but Tabitha scurried away.

I ripped open the box. My glasses were inside! I had never been so excited to receive something that was already mine.

"Yay! My beautiful, old glasses," I said. I kissed the case dramatically. They were much better than my broken pair, even if the prescription was a little bit off. I was filled with joy for the rest of the day. I was so happy to have un-taped glasses.

"I heard it will only be another day or two until the cabin wall is fixed," Aries said to me on our short walk back from dinner. They served our sandwiches in the Mess Hall now. The power was still out, but it was kind of nice to sit around all the other campers. Even if we were in the dark.

"And then we'll be back to normal. Well, sort of," I answered. I looked around the semi-dark campgrounds. Holly and Tara bumped into each other. They pretended they couldn't see in the dark.

"They seem extra rowdy tonight, don't you think?" Aries asked. "It's sort of like they've got something up their sleeves." She gestured toward Holly and Tara. Charlie overheard us and joined the conversation.

"I don't know," Charlie said. "It's so hard to tell with those two." We learned that Aries was right later that night.

"Guess what I have, everyone?" Holly called out after we returned from another lackluster dinner. We all watched as Holly pulled out a box out from under her cot.

"Please tell me you have a puppy!" Buffy shrieked. She clapped her hands excitedly. "That would make this stupid storm a gazillion times better."

"No! It's not a puppy. Or any living creature," Holly said. She wanted us to guess again.

"Is it a generator?" Aries asked. She was only half-joking. "It would have to be a small one, though, because the box isn't that big." Holly sharply shook her head. She quickly dismissed Aries' comment.

"Is that a care package?" Marla asked. "I could really use some chocolate."

"No, this was just a leftover box *from* a care package," Holly snapped. Her patience was wearing thin.

"Oh, just tell us!" Janice shouted. She leaned over to see what was in the box. She accidentally fell off her bed. "Ow!" she cried. She rubbed her elbow as she got up.

"Well . . ." Holly began dramatically. "Since the storm started, Tara and I have 'collected' food from the Mess Hall."

"Food rationing! That's smart," Aries said. She nodded her head in approval.

"We're not trying to be rational, silly," Tara laughed. "This is for something fun!" Aries looked like she was about to correct Tara. She kept her mouth shut, though.

"Ladies, we are going to challenge the Goldfinches to a food fight!" Holly exclaimed. She threw containers of Jell-O, applesauce, and other food packets in the air. "Put your raincoats on and let's go! We need to do this before Tabitha comes back."

"We already checked with some of the 'Finches and they're up for it," Tara said. She glanced over at Charlie.

"You're sure the Goldfinches agreed?" Charlie asked. She eyed Holly carefully.

"Yes. Totally," Holly said. I wasn't sure I believed her. Most of the girls put on their rain ponchos and boots. I reflexively touched the frame of my replacement glasses. They reminded me of Holly's last prank.

"C'mon, Noodle! You only live once," Aries whispered. She saw my hesitation. "What else are we going to do? It's not like Tabitha is going to lead us in a charades marathon." I put on my rain gear with a shrug. I might come up with a good bit for my radio show. *If* I got back on the air before the first session ended.

Holly didn't think of two key details. First, she didn't check to see how heavy the box was. She also didn't realize that cardboard and rain don't mix. We had only walked about twenty feet from the Rec Center when the box started to fall apart in Buffy and Tara's hands.

"I don't think we'll make it up to the Goldfinches' cabin in this rain," Tara said. She glanced up the hill.

"Yeah, and my arms kind of hurt," Buffy added. She put her end of the box on the ground. "Let's just have our own food fight."

"Yeah! We can do it over there," Tara said. She pointed to a nearby cluster of trees. She and Buffy half-carried, half-dragged the box over toward the trees. Holly scowled at the soggy box that had foiled her plan. No one else cared, though, and it didn't take long before the food started flying.

"Take that, Hurricane Hilda!" Buffy shrieked. She sprayed a pouch of applesauce in the air like a hose. Tara tossed an oatmeal packet like it was confetti. Holly quickly recovered from her disappointment. She dumped chocolate pudding on Charlie's head. Charlie responded by hurling two handfuls of Jell-O back at Holly. I got hit on the cheek with either Jell-O, pudding, or some combination of both.

"Aaaaaahhhhh!" Aries shrieked. She ran toward Buffy and Holly. She squirted grape jelly packets from her fingers. I watched everyone scream and laugh. I smiled. The past few days had been hard. We lost our counselor and our cabin. It rained nonstop. But we still had each other. This wacky bunch of girls had become my friends. When I first got here, I never thought that I would have felt this way. I guess Holly and Tara's pranks had brought us closer together.

Holly and Tara hadn't collected that much ammunition. It only took a few minutes to use up our food fight supplies. When the food ran out, some of the girls still tried to scoop up handfuls of oatmeal from the ground to throw in the air.

"You guys, this is getting gross," Marla complained. A clump of grassy oatmeal hit her square in the face. "There's dirt in the oatmeal that you're throwing! We've already taken showers."

"Okay, we'll stop," Holly said. She threw one last chunk of a "Jell-Oat" mixture at Tara. We were exhausted. We all balanced delicately on a semi-dry tree stump to catch our breath.

"See? Wasn't that fun?" Holly asked. She wiped away a glob of Aries' jelly from her forehead.

"That was amazing," Tara responded. She licked the back of her hand. "Man, I love chocolate pudding."

"Eww, Tara, don't eat that!" Charlie shouted. She batted Tara's hand down. "That might be mud. Or something worse." Tara shrugged. She wiped her hand on her poncho instead.

"You know, I've never had more fun getting chocolate pudding in my eye," I said. As I wiped my forehead, a huge glob of pudding plopped to the ground.

"Yeah, I hear grape jelly is great for your hair," Aries added. "Makes it super shiny."

"And super sticky," I said, touching my own hair. We all laughed. It was such an amazing feeling, being together in the pouring rain. The forest food fight would definitely be one of my favorite camp memories.

"I'm really glad I met you guys." The words came out of my mouth before I could take them back. *Oh well,* I thought. *Too late now.* "I wouldn't want to go through a hurricane with anyone else."

"Yeah," Charlie piped up. "Same here."

Aries squeezed my hand. "Me too."

"Could you imagine what camp would've been like without Hurricane Hilda?" Buffy said. "So boooriiiinnnggg!"

"Soooo boring," Tara said. She put her arm around Buffy's shoulders and gave Buffy a gentle shake.

"Sandpipers forever!" Janice shouted. We all screamed "Sandpipers forever" a few times and high-fived each other. Eventually, we tired of cheering, but nobody wanted to move. As we sat together on the stump, we watched the rain fall. A quiet peace settled over us.

"OK. So how are we going to get all this food off of us?" Marla eventually asked. She tried to clean her face with a corner of her dirty poncho. "You're only supposed to leave an oatmeal mask on for a few minutes. Even if it *is* partly a mud mask."

"We'll just wash off in the bathroom," Holly answered. She pointed to the nearby bathrooms we had to use while we stayed at the Rec Center.

"We can leave the ponchos outside in the rain. Maybe they'll get cleaned off. A couple of hours in this downpour and our ponchos will be as clean as a whistle tomorrow morning. Just like a washing machine," Tara said. She smiled confidently. We were all too tired to tell her otherwise.

Chapter 16

A NIGHTTIME VISITOR

We took turns rinsing off in the darkened bathroom by the light of Aries' flashlight. We let Marla go first. She claimed that she had the most to wash off. Thankfully, we cleaned up quickly. "Wait. Where should we leave these sticky ponchos?" Buffy asked before we went back to the Rec Center. "I don't want to get dirty all over again."

"Let's spread them out on the picnic tables outside," Tara said. She motioned toward an area outside the bathrooms between the Rec Center and the Mess Hall. We laid down our ponchos in a row. Charlie and Janice hung their ponchos on some hooks they found nearby.

We snuck back into the Rec Center. Aries poked her head down the basement steps to see if Tabitha was waiting for us.

"I bet Tabitha hasn't stepped foot in here since *yesterday's* cabin clean-up," Holly said. She wore a satisfied smile. We all ignored her.

We were surprisingly tired after all the excitement. We fell asleep quickly for the first time in four days. I wasn't sure how long we'd been asleep, but Aries sat straight up in bed sometime around two in the morning.

"What's that sound? Did anyone else hear that sound?" she asked. Her voice was strained in a scared whisper.

"What sound?" Buffy asked. She rubbed her eyes and straightened her "Cat-tastrophe" pajama top. It had a picture of a cat stuck in a tree on the front.

"That scratching sound!" Aries said. She gestured wildly toward the stairs and the Rec Center door. "Can't you hear it?" Those of us who had woken up craned our necks. We looked where Aries pointed. She was pointing to where we'd hung up our ponchos.

"It sounds like it's coming closer," I said as calmly as I could. I didn't want anyone to panic. I guess it didn't come out the way I had hoped because Buffy freaked out.

"Oh my goodness! Everyone, hide!" Buffy shrieked. She pulled the covers over her head.

"Relax. We're in the basement, you guys," Holly said. "Nothing's coming down here." No one pointed out that animals could easily walk down some stairs. Except for cows, maybe, but that seemed like something I should keep to myself.

"Where's Tabitha?" Janice asked. "She should be here to help us!"

"Oh, like all the other times she's helped us," Aries said. She shook her head sarcastically.

"Well, *someone* should go out and check," Janice responded.

"Not me!" Marla said first. I'm sure someone shot Marla an irritated glance. I know I did.

"What happens if we see something? Who are we going to tell?" Charlie asked. She took her turn as the bunk's voice of reason.

"We just need to take a peek outside to see what we're dealing with," Aries said. "Then we can figure out what to do. So, who wants to be the one to go out and look?" The only response that Aries got was the *pitter-patter* of the rain. "Fine! I'll go," she added in a huff.

"Aries, I'll go with you," I found myself saying. I grabbed my tennis racket just in case. I'm glad I thought the racket was essential when we left the Sandpipers' cabin.

"Are you bringing that racket so you and the boogeyman can play a mixed doubles match?" Holly said. She laughed at her own joke. I decided to ignore her.

"Be careful," Buffy called out softly as we crept upstairs. We went out the door. Aries and I pressed up against the outside wall of the Rec Center. We walked as quietly as we could in squeaky wet rainboots. When we rounded the corner, Aries (who, thankfully, was in the lead) let out a sharp hiss.

"Move, move, move!" Aries whispered. Her eyes were wide with fear. "It's a bear!" We stumbled in our clunky boots. We managed to get back into the Rec Center and slam the door. Aries stood against the door. She held it closed even though it was already tightly shut.

"That was fast," Holly remarked casually when we ran back down into the basement. She didn't seem to care that we had just risked our lives.

"There's a bear out there, you guys. He's licking our ponchos!" Aries screamed. She was nearly hysterical.

"The bear could be a 'she,' you know," Marla remarked with a shrug. "I'm just saying!" she added when Aries glared at her.

"A bear? No way! I don't believe you," Holly said. She shook her head in disbelief as she tried to look out of the tiny basement window.

"It was a big brown bear, with giant paws," Aries said. She was still in shock. I hadn't seen anything, but I believed Aries.

"At least it wasn't another snake," Janice joked. I would've made a wisecrack just like that if I hadn't been nearly face-to-face with a bear.

"You're sure it was a bear?" Charlie asked. She clutched a boot in her hand, presumably for protection. "Not just a large raccoon?"

"I know what a bear looks like!" Aries snapped.

"Well, whatever it was, it must have been hungry," Buffy remarked with a shrug. "Those ponchos were covered in food."

"Shouldn't we warn somebody?" Charlie asked. "Tabitha's still out there somewhere, right?"

"I'll wait by the front door to look out for Tabitha . . . or anybody who might come by," I said. I suddenly felt brave. "And I'll make sure no bears get inside."

"You'll need to make noise if there's a bear," Aries said. She rustled around in her trunk. She was looking for something. "When I went to Yellowstone National Park, I had a walking stick with bells on it. The jingling sound scared the bears away.

I don't have the walking stick with me, but hopefully this will do." Aries pulled out a noisemaker like the kind they give out at kid's birthday parties.

"I won't even ask why you have that, Aries De Falco," I said. I shook my head. I took a deep breath and readied myself for guard duty.

Chapter 17

TABITHA'S BRIGHTER SIDE

I stayed alert for what felt like an hour, but my eyes grew heavier with each blink. I was so tired that I leaned against the Rec Center door. I just wanted to sleep. But then I heard a rustling outside. What could be making that noise? I couldn't see anything when I looked through the window, so I grabbed my tennis racket. I took a few deep breaths to calm myself down. *Please don't be a bear, please don't be a bear*, I thought as I flung open the door. I swung the racket blindly in front of me. Fortunately, I didn't hit anything.

"Jeez, Noodle!" Tabitha exclaimed in a sharp whisper. She dropped all the ponchos she had gathered. "Are you trying to kill me?"

"I, uh, um," I sputtered. "I was keeping watch for a bear . . . or you . . . or anyone . . . to tell them about the bear."

"There was a bear here?" Tabitha asked. She cocked her head to the side in disbelief. "Of course there was. These ponchos smell like the Mess Hall garbage cans! Didn't Bob and Dotty tell you not to keep food near the cabin? It's like you guys had a food fight the way these jackets stink." She paused for a moment. "Wait . . . did you guys have a food fight?"

"Ummm," I stalled. I tried to think about how to best respond. "A little?" I added, bending over to pick up a poncho that had fallen again.

"You're kidding, right?" Tabitha said, her eyes narrowing as I guiltily drew a circle out of a water droplet on the floor with my foot. "Oh, jeez! You're not kidding. I could get fired for letting you get out in the middle of the storm." Tabitha motioned for me to come outside.

"Well, if *you* had been here, maybe we wouldn't have been outside," I said. I closed the door carefully, so I didn't wake everyone up. I kept my eyes on Tabitha. She had a hard time holding all the wet ponchos. I couldn't help but grab a couple that fell. *Darn it*, I silently cursed myself. *Don't aid the enemy!*

"I . . . I . . . had some important things to do," Tabitha stammered. She spoke a softer tone that I had never heard before. *Stay tough*, I told myself.

"What could be more important than watching us during a hurricane? There's no power! We aren't even teenagers yet!" I said.

"It's just . . . something I needed to do," Tabitha sputtered weakly. After a moment, the old Tabitha came back to her senses and her tone shifted. "Let's make a deal: you don't tell on me and I don't tell on you. I'm sure you can convince the rest of the girls. After all, it's in their best interests, too."

"Well, I don't know," I said slowly. I was still trying to be tough. Shelby's advice echoed in my ears: "Tabitha's your counselor and deserves your respect." I scratched one of the many bug bites on my arm as I considered her offer.

"Please?" Tabitha asked again. She talked in a voice that actually made her sound more human. I could hardly believe it. Tabitha, who was so cold and standoffish, suddenly seemed . . . vulnerable. *Wait until the girls hear about this!* I thought.

"If you cover for me, Noodle," Tabitha continued before I had a chance to speak, "I promise you won't regret it." Whatever Tabitha was hiding must have been a big deal.

"Okay, fine. It's a deal," I said, wearily. After all, I was pretty tired.

"We should *properly* clean off these ponchos. We don't want the animals to come back and eat them for dessert," Tabitha said. "I know there's a hose outside the Mess Hall."

"Okay," I said. I tried to stifle a yawn. I didn't want to go anywhere but to bed.

"You know what? I can handle this on my own. You should go to sleep," Tabitha said. This was a gesture of kindness that I had never seen from her before. I tried to muster a smile that showed my appreciation.

"Goodnight, Tabitha," I said. "And thank you." Tabitha gave me a slight nod. It was so slight that I may have imagined it. When I slunk back downstairs, only Aries was still awake.

"What happened? Did you see the bear?" Aries asked. "Are we in trouble?"

"It's all good," I said. I climbed onto my cot. "I have no idea where Tabitha was, but we both agreed that we would keep quiet about each of us breaking the rules."

"Really?" Aries said. "I wonder what she's up to."

"Whatever Tabitha was doing must have been a pretty big deal to her. She's cleaning off the ponchos for us. I don't know what got into her, but she actually seemed . . . kind of nice. For Tabitha, at least."

"I wish I knew what she has up her sleeve. That would be good information to have . . . just in case," Aries said. She looked out to the tiny window above our heads, trying to see Tabitha. One downside of the basement Rec Center was the terrible view.

"To be continued another time," I said. "I'm exhausted."

I woke up the next morning to Aries quietly humming while playing a game of solitaire.

"Happy Thursday," Aries said, glancing over at me. "It's raining. Again. And we still have no power." That meant that muffins, bagels, and cold cereal were probably the breakfast choices for the day. I dreamed of a plate piled high with steaming scrambled eggs and ketchup. Ketchup made everything taste a million times better.

"Ugh! When are we going to get the power back? I hate these boring breakfasts!" Marla complained.

"It's got to be soon," Charlie answered. She looked out the window to check the weather for herself. "They can't keep running a camp on ice cubes. Can they?" Before the girls could debate the menu options or how miserable the weather was, Tabitha burst in.

"Rise-n-shine, 'Pipers! Another gloomy day at Camp Hillside awaits," she called out. She sounded like her old self.

"On today's agenda, after reveille and breakfast, we have indoor bowling and greeting card-making. There's also knitting, which I hear is 'sew' much fun. Get it? 'S-E-W'?" Only Buffy laughed heartily.

"What? I can appreciate a good pun, okay?" Buffy said defensively. She pointed to her green top. It had a picture of a tea bag and the words "Green 'T'-Shirt" underneath.

"What's gotten into Tabitha today?" Charlie whispered to me. "She's acting strange."

"You mean stranger than usual?" I whispered back. We both giggled. "I think something may have changed after I ran into her last night. I'll fill you in later." Tabitha motioned for us to head toward the door before I could say anything else.

"Come on! Your delicious cold breakfast awaits," Tabitha said. Something was definitely different about Tabitha. We filed out for our quick trip to the Mess Hall. We saw our ponchos hanging neatly from a clothesline someone had strung underneath the Rec Center's porch. We all "oohed" and "aahed" at the sight of Tabitha's handiwork.

"You girls did a terrible job cleaning those ponchos," Tabitha said with a shrug. "I figured you could use a hand."

"Oh wow, Tabitha," Charlie exclaimed. "That's really nice of you. Isn't that really nice of Tabitha, you guys?"

"Yeah, it *is* nice," I added. I followed Charlie's lead. The other girls chimed in with varying degrees of enthusiasm. I swear I saw a flicker of a smile from Tabitha. It didn't last long.

"Well, don't get used to it," Tabitha responded gruffly. "Besides, I didn't want to have to smell you all day long." The new and slightly improved Tabitha seemed to take her counselor role a little more seriously. At least for the moment.

Chapter 18

HURRICANE HILDA IS HISTORY

After Tabitha's random act of kindness, camp life seemed to take a turn for the . . . *better*. The rain had slowed. We were finally able to go outside without our ponchos. And the best news of all? On Friday morning, Bob told us that we could finally move back into our cabin after lunch.

"Ladies, you will need to do a major clean up before you leave," Dotty advised. "All the dirty clothes make it look like we have wall-to-wall carpeting down here," she added. She held up one of Buffy's shirts that said "Fry Day" for emphasis. Anyone could probably guess what picture was on the front. As we packed up the last of our things, we heard a short crackle. Then there was a sudden burst of light. Aries was the first to realize what had happened.

"The power is back on!" she screamed. The entire Rec Center basement erupted in cheers.

"The power is back! The power is back! Hallelujah, the power is back!" we sang. We danced around in a circle. As we laughed and cheered together, I suddenly felt sad. Would the closeness that had grown between us over the past few days end once we moved back to our old cabin? I hoped not. Even Holly and Tara seemed a little bit nicer. Though not by much.

As we waited for the van to load up our belongings, I had a few minutes to write my parents a letter.

Friday, July 17

Dear Mommy and Daddy,

I meant to write to you sooner, but things have been busy. Thank you so much for having Mrs. Pearson mail my glasses!! I'll write her a thank you note, I promise. It was the best care package ever. I do love all the books and magazines you have sent, though. In even more exciting news, the power just came back on! Hurricane Hilda is history.

I have so much to tell you, but my hand is cramping from all the writing I've been doing. I can't believe camp is over in nine days. We're supposed to have a big luau later to celebrate the end of the storm. I wonder if they'll serve tornadoes of beef . . . or sunny-side up eggs . . . or maybe even blackout chocolate cake—ha! And Tabitha, our "substitute counselor," might not be so bad. I don't know for sure yet, though. Keep your fingers crossed that the radio station will be up and running soon. I have been working on my material nonstop. I could probably do two hours with all that I've written, but I hope to have at least five minutes.

Okay, I'll write again soon. If I have time. :-)

S.S.S. (Sorry So Sloppy).
Love, Noodle

Charlie and Janice made our big return to the cabin even more dramatic. They announced that they were trading bunks with Marla and Buffy. That meant that they were moving closer to Aries and me. And Marla and Buffy would be moving closer to Holly and Tara.

"Now I can hear your stories better, Noodle," Charlie whispered to me.

"And I won't trip on as many things on my way to the bathroom," Janice added. This meant that the other girls had officially accepted Aries and I as Sandpipers. The wall next to Tara and Holly's bed had been patched up and painted. The brightly-painted wall looked weird compared to the rest of the old cabin.

"Alright, 'Pipers, now that we're all back to normal . . . or whatever all of this is," Tabitha said. She waved her hand at the newly arranged the room. "Let's get to the Mess Hall for the big luau dinner. It's finally safe to drink milk and eat potato salad again!"

"Thank goodness. I am so sick of having bug juice at every meal," Marla said. She flipped her hair like Holly and Tara sometimes did. Marla's hair wasn't as long as theirs, so the flip didn't have the same effect.

"I bet she still drinks bug juice tonight," Holly whispered to Tara. Tara just shrugged. She was probably still thinking about potato salad. I know I was. I couldn't wait to have something other than a sandwich or cereal. Dinner that night didn't disappoint. The chicken was covered in a pineapple-teriyaki sauce. It tasted so good. After dinner, Bob and Dotty got up on the stage. They were wearing matching Hawaiian outfits.

"Aloha, campers!" Bob's voice boomed over the sound system. "It's lovely to be back onstage with a working microphone and these beautiful, bright lights." Bob covered his eyes with his hand. The spotlight moved down a little. "Dotty and I wanted to thank each of you for your patience and cooperation during the storm." Dotty clapped at the audience. She made a wide circle with her hands. Dotty reminded me of Mrs. King, my favorite teacher. Mrs. King made the same gesture when she gave students a round of applause.

"You all deserve a big hand for sticking together. You showed your best Camp Hillside selves during a very challenging time," Dotty added. "Tomorrow morning, we will return to our regular camp schedule!" Someone let out a loud whistle at the back of the Mess Hall. Another girl shouted, "Woohoo!" A bunch of other girls cheered, too. It was hard to contain our energy. It felt like we had been cooped up forever. I covered my ears and screamed along with everyone else. It finally felt like camp.

By Tuesday, the storm was just a memory. There were still several patches of mud on the ground as a final reminder. Tuesday was also the day we were scheduled to go back on the radio.

"We leave for Radio 'Ill-side' in five minutes!" Tabitha announced.

"Maybe the repair crew fixed the station's sign right after they fixed our cabin," I said. I readied a stack of my material.

"Doubt it," replied Charlie. "I think the broken gate at the horse stables is higher priority. I'm pretty sure Silver and Thumper are going to escape if it's not repaired."

"Don't forget the rickety ladder at the dock," Aries added. She leaped down from her bunk.

"I'm sure everything will be exactly the same. Come on. Let's go, girls," Tabitha said. She pointed to the clock. We made pretty good time getting to the radio station because it wasn't raining on us.

Clay met us at the radio station door with an excited wave. He pointed to a flattened cardboard box pathway that was supposed to help keep the carpet clean. Sadly, he was about ten years too late for that. I got out my papers. I flipped through them to remind myself of what I had prepared. I didn't really need to, but it felt good to refresh myself before I went on.

"Okay. Who's up first today?" Clay asked as he flipped on a few buttons and switches. Didn't he remember what happened the last time we were at the radio station? I guess a lot had happened since we had been here just over a week ago.

"Tara and I will go first," Holly said. She linked her arms with Tara's. *No, no, no!* I wanted to scream. They can't do this to me!

"Noodle's up first! Don't you remember?" Aries asked. She firmly eyed Holly and Tara. The station suddenly felt hot. My head started pounding. It felt like it might explode.

"That was *Shelby's* rule," Holly said. She didn't back down from Aries' glare. "Now that Tabitha's here, it doesn't really matter anymore. Right, Tabitha?" Tabitha looked up from the magazine she'd been reading and shrugged her shoulders.

"I don't know what promises were made, but you should figure it out quickly," Tabitha said. "This isn't a twenty-four-hour station." *Oh no. Oh no.* Why couldn't Tabitha act more like a counselor? We didn't have the time to argue. I'd waited for so long to redeem myself. No! I refused to let Holly ruin this moment for me.

"*I* was supposed to go first," I insisted. I hoped someone other than Aries would back me up. Tabitha looked around. It was like she was curious to see what was going to happen next. *Please, Tabitha, say something*, I begged in my head. *Somebody say something.*

"They're right. Noodle *was* supposed to go first," Charlie said. She nodded her head slowly. "That was the plan after Aries wanted to be the engineer and messed everything up. Sorry, Aries."

"Don't remind me," Aries mumbled. She stared sheepishly at the floor. The other girls looked at Holly. They waited to see how she would respond. Holly turned and looked at me with venom in her eyes.

I stared right back at Holly. I was not backing down.

"Okay! Fine," Holly said with an annoyed sigh. "But I—I mean, *we*—are going on second." Holly gestured to Tara and Marla. They were huddled around a scrap of paper and writing down song choices. Unlike Shelby, Tabitha wasn't much help in managing our cabin's "personalities." Instead, Tabitha just kept reading her magazine. She did a pretty good job of tuning us out.

"Great. Let's get the show on the road," Tabitha said dryly. She didn't look up.

"Um, Clay, are you going to put on the timer again so that we all can see how much time is left?" Holly looked directly at me as she said the word "we." I wasn't going to let her rattle me right before I went on. Clay cleared his throat. He nodded at Holly slightly but otherwise ignored her.

"Alright. Noodle's up first," Clay said as he motioned me over. "And Aries, I can show you *some* of the controls," he added. "But not everything. I've still got to keep my job." Aries looked almost as pleased as me.

"But what about the rest of us who are waiting?" Marla grumbled. "Do we get to learn the control thingies, too?"

"Some other time, maybe?" Clay said. "I think this is just for the folks who aren't going on air."

"Don't worry, Marla," Charlie said. "That just means you'll have more time to prepare 'Marla's Mega-Mix.'" Marla nodded. Still, the lingering purse of her lips showed that she wasn't completely satisfied.

"You got this, Noodle," Clay said to me. He turned his hat around backwards as he put on his headphones. I nodded and forced a smile. I tried not to think about my last disaster on air. Clay smiled back and pointed to the booth.

After I got settled, Clay and Aries signaled that it was time to begin. Aries shadowed Clay's every move. I could feel the other girls' eyes on me. I'm sure they wondered if I would choke again. I didn't dare look at Holly. For some reason, I heard my sister's voice in my head. She said, "You'll have the chance to be whoever you want to be. Oh man, you're going to looooove sleepaway camp."

"Break a leg," Aries mouthed to me. The "On Air" light turned on and Clay signaled for everyone to be quiet. I swallowed and took a breath. This was it. I had to step up. I opened my mouth to speak. Once I got going, it was hard to stop.

"Good afternoon, Camp Hillside. This is Noodle Newman from the Sandpipers' cabin coming to you live from a puddle outside the Mess Hall. I'm only kidding! My soggy socks and I are broadcasting to you from Radio Hillside." I could see everyone smiling at me. Well, mostly everyone. I was nervous, but also excited. This time felt different. Aries gave me a big thumb's up. So long, Sad Old Noodle. Hello, Radio Noodle!

"Seriously! I thought my first time at camp was going to be a washout because of homesickness, not because of a storm. A big thank you to Hurricane Hilda for that," I said. I hardly had to glance down at my notes. I had never felt so happy as I continued through the material I had prepared. I felt so energized. It was like a jolt of lightning had gone through me.

I saw the Sandpipers laughing. I could tell that anyone else who was listening was probably laughing at all the right places, too.

Tara whispered something excitedly to Holly. Holly just shrugged. Aries told me later that Tara had said that she couldn't believe how good I was.

Before I knew it, Clay signaled that it was time to take a break. I wanted to stay on for longer. I now understood why Holly was so bossy about her airtime.

"Girl, you were on fire!" Buffy remarked. She thumped me on the back so hard I almost coughed up my lunch. Marla smiled politely, but she wasted no time slipping past me to get into the booth. Holly and Tara followed close behind.

"Great job, Noodle," Tara whispered on her way in. She gave me a gentle punch on my shoulder. "You were super funny."

"Noodle, you were fantastic," Charlie whispered. She gave me a tight hug. I have no idea what happened while the rest of the bunk had their time. I was too busy walking on air.

While we were leaving the station, Clay called me over. He held a phone in his hand.

"Noodle, it's for you," he said. He handed me the phone. "It's Bob," he mouthed. He attempted to look serious.

"Um, hello?" I asked.

"Noodle Newman!" the voice boomed. "Bob here, of Bob and Dotty fame." Bob took a moment to chuckle at his own joke. "Listen, I wanted to chat more with you later. Things have been a bit bananas now that Hurricane Hilda has finally left us. I hoped to catch you quickly now . . ." I glanced up. I hoped no one was paying attention to our conversation. No such luck. The entire cabin, Tabitha, and Clay were watching me. They strained to hear the conversation. We all had no idea why Bob had called.

"Oh yes, I'm sure you're very busy," I said. I circled my finger around a stain on the desk left by Clay's coffee cup.

"Well, listen, Miss Newman," Bob continued. "Dotty and I heard you on the radio. All we can say is, 'Wow!' followed by another, 'Wow!' You were unbelievable, young lady. Just fantastic. Dotty and I were floored by your on-air performance."

"Thank you," I said. My cheeks flushed.

"Listen, you were such a natural. Dotty and I were wondering if you might be interested in having some more airtime next summer. Maybe your own show. That is, if we're lucky enough to have you back. No need to answer now! We just wanted to give you something to think about."

"Thank you, sir," I said. "I am pretty sure my answer will be a 'yes,' but I'll think about it."

"Okay, super," Bob said. Noodle heard another telephone line ring in the background. "Listen, Miss Newman, duty calls. Think about it. Ciao for now." Bob hung up the phone. Before I had a chance to say thank you or goodbye. I stared at the phone for a second. I processed what had just happened before I hung it up.

"Yay, Noodle!" Aries exclaimed. She ran over to give me a hug. "Bob's kind of a loud talker. We all heard your conversation with him." The rest of the girls shared their congratulations, too. Even Holly said something, but I don't think she really meant it. I couldn't wait to send my mom and dad a letter. I got so caught up in having fun that I didn't remember to write my parents until the final Wednesday of camp.

Wednesday, July 22

Dear Mom and Dad,

I hope you didn't think that I got stuck in the mud since I haven't written to you in a few days. Everything is nearly dried out and camp is getting back to "normal." Well, normal for camp. I finally had my turn on air, and I absolutely NAILED IT. It went so well that Bob asked me to do a special radio show next summer. As if I can wait until next summer. But I guess I'll have to.

Oh, and while we were eating breakfast in the Mess Hall, this older camper came over and asked which one of us was

Noodle. The girl said, "You totally rocked it on air the other day," and then walked away. I couldn't believe it! I tried to play it cool and just say, "Thanks." I didn't want the other girls to be jealous. Inside, I was bursting with joy.

Anyway, I'm super busy now with all the activities that we couldn't do in the rain. I have had so many ideas for stories and material if I had another chance at the radio show. But that probably won't happen since you pick me up on Sunday ☹. We also have a camp carnival coming up on Saturday. It's supposed to be really fun. Anyway, I've got to go since Shower Hour is almost over. I got ready in five minutes today.

Sun-cerely yours (Get it? The weather is
so much nicer when it's not a hurricane),
Noodle

I sealed the envelope. I only smudged the "G" in Great Falls this time. It's not easy being left-handed in a mostly right-handed world. I remembered what I wrote about having to wait until next summer for the radio show. I kind of felt sad. Why couldn't Bob and Dotty come up with a special slot for me right now? Why did I have to wait until next summer? What if I didn't come back to Camp Hillside?

I couldn't imagine going to another camp after all that happened this summer. How could I survive without Aries' wisecracks, Charlie's kindness, Buffy's silly shirts, Janice's goofiness, Tara's crazy antics, and even Marla's complaining? Maybe Holly would grow up a little. Maybe she'd be a little nicer to me next year.

Camp had been full of surprises so far. When I woke up the next morning, I learned that Holly still had one more surprise up her sleeve.

"Listen up, Sandpipers!" Holly clapped her hands to get our attention during Cabin Clean-up on Friday morning. "As you know, we have exactly three full days left in the first session." Holly waited until everyone stopped what they were doing before she continued. I didn't need much convincing to take a break from cleaning up. Even if it meant listening to Holly. "I've thought of one last thing we can do to shake things up before some of you head home."

"Tell us, tell us!" Tara said. She jumped up and down on the bed she had just made. What a waste of a nicely made bed.

"Okay, here's the plan," Holly began. She whispered loudly. I'm sure anyone within a five-mile radius could hear Holly's voice. "Tomorrow afternoon, we will sneak onto Radio Hillside and take over the air waves. Old people would call it 'pirate radio'!" It took me a moment to figure out what Holly meant by pirate radio. At first, I thought of a parrot by a microphone saying "Ahoy, matey!" Then I thought about how pirate radio didn't seem like a good idea. Thank goodness I wasn't the first one to point this out.

"Uh, that sounds kind of dangerous," Marla said. She pursed her lips in disapproval.

"Come on, girls! Think of how fun it will be to go on air again," Holly said. She completely ignored Marla. Her eyes paused on me for an extra half second when she looked my way. I don't think she had ever looked directly at me before, not including her glares and stares. "If we can pull this off, the Sandpipers will become camp legends."

"Yeah, legends!" Tara said with forced enthusiasm. I noticed that she had stopped bouncing on her bed.

"We've got to get Noodle back on air one last time," Holly said. She locked eyes with me. It was like Holly thought I'd do anything to go back on the air one last time. How did she know? Oh no! Was she reading my mind?

"But can't we just wait for our turn?" Marla asked. This was ironic because she was perhaps the least patient person I knew.

"Yeah, Bob did promise Noodle her special show . . ." Charlie added.

"That show isn't until *next* summer," Holly said. She scanned our faces. "Who knows what the bunks will be next year? Someone might not come back. We may never all be together again." She did have a point there.

"But do we really need to *sneak* on the air? Isn't there another way?" I asked. I wracked my brain for another solution that wouldn't break so many rules. "Maybe we could just *ask* Bob and Dotty if we could go on."

"Oh, please. They would never agree to that," Holly snapped. "Come on! Live a little before you leave. You owe it to yourself . . . after your 'difficult' start at camp and all." Holly was so sneaky. She knew that if I agreed to her plan, everyone else would agree, too. Even more, I hated that I was starting to fall for it!

"What's the worst they could do to you? Send you home?" Tara asked. She did have a point there.

"It'll be in and out—ten minutes on air, tops," Holly said. Oh, those ten-minute promises. Where have I heard that before? "After that, we'll go right to the carnival . . ." Holly paused for dramatic effect. Then she added, ". . . But we'll go as *radio heroes*." Holly put her hands together. She was begging me to say yes. She could sense that I was cracking. *Ugh*. I was torn. On the one hand, it would be great to go on air one last time before I left. On the other hand, was it worth the risk?

"Say yes, Noodle," Aries whispered to me. "Do it . . . for all of us."

"Well," I said, sighing heavily. "I don't know . . ."

"Yes, you do know. You want to say 'yes!'" Holly exclaimed. Holly knew that I had caved when I didn't immediately protest. "There. It's settled. We're going on. We'll do it tomorrow after lunch, during our siesta. Everyone will be getting ready for the carnival." Holly gave me a triumphant nod. She sealed the deal for a decision that I had somehow made on the entire bunk's behalf.

"Oh, boy," Buffy muttered. "What are we getting ourselves into *now*?" Holly put her fingers to her lips as we heard Tabitha clunking up the cabin steps outside.

"Hey, 'Pipers," Tabitha called. She knocked on the window before she yanked open the door. "Hope you finished your clean up! It's time for swim." She glanced at her watch and added, "Oops. You only have five minutes to make it to the Great Lake." It took at least ten minutes just to make it down the hill. We would all be late. We grabbed our goggles and towels and rushed out the door. I still pretended Shelby was leading us. In my head I said, "Give me your left, left, your left, right, left."

"I'll see you all later!" Marla called. She skipped off when we passed the Arts and Crafts Studio. This was her new favorite place to hang out whenever we went swimming. Marla was pretty sharp. The Arts and Crafts Studio was one of the few buildings with air conditioning.

"It may not be so bad to sneak onto the radio, you know," Aries said to me after the Sandpipers dropped off Marla. We were all hurrying down to the Great Lake so that we'd have extra time to catch with Kurt the Flirt and his dazzling green eyes.

"What do you mean?" I asked. I hoped Aries had a clever solution to Holly's proposal.

"Well," Aries began, "You're going home on Sunday, right? So, they really can't punish you if we get caught. The rest of the girls who are staying for the whole summer might be in a jam, but *you* don't have to worry about that."

"I would feel guilty if everyone else got in trouble because of me," I said. "It just doesn't feel right."

"Okay, well . . . what if Bob forgets about giving you your own show next summer? Why not give yourself one extra time on air with Holly's last hurrah?" Aries asked. "Assuming you're coming back, of course." We had not talked about our plans for next summer. Four weeks ago, I never imagined that I would have this conversation.

"You think I want to go somewhere new after all that's happened? No way!" I said. I playfully punched Aries on the shoulder. "But what about you?"

"Well, I would come back solely to keep you out of trouble," Aries said with a laugh. Then she turned serious. "But a lot can happen in a year. I mean, who knows? Maybe I'll get a job. Or maybe my dad will suddenly have other plans for me next summer—even though this was the first summer that I've ever been happy."

"Do you really think your dad wouldn't let you come back?" I asked. I couldn't imagine camp without Aries. I also knew that stories don't always have happy endings. She shrugged.

"Let's just take a chance, Noodle," Aries said. "Besides, if you go on air, then I'll get to try out the control boards on my own." As an afterthought, she added, "It would almost be like we would do it for Shelby . . . to show her how far we've come."

Wait! Doing it for Shelby? My ears pricked up at this suggestion. Sneaking onto the radio with a purpose seemed much better than sneaking on just for kicks!

A thought popped into my head as we walked back to our cabin from the lake later that day. "Aries, what if Holly's got something else planned for when we sneak onto the radio?" I asked. "What if she double-crosses us?" Aries scrunched up her face and cocked her head sideways.

"You may be right. Something tells me that Holly hasn't thought her plan through too deeply," Aries said. She added, "But remember, you'll be the one with the microphone and I'll be the one at the controls. I would say we have the power."

"Do it as a tribute to Shelby. That's a very interesting idea." I mumbled. My mind wandered. Where was my notepad when I needed it? I suddenly had a bunch of ideas to write down. I snatched up my notebook as we walked into the cabin. I flipped to the next blank page. *Only two pages left?!* I thought to myself. I had to figure out how to write down all of my ideas with so little space.

"Wakey, wakey, eggs and bake-y! It's Carnival Day," Tabitha said on Saturday morning. She greeted me by roughly shaking my feet. She seemed . . . happy. It was like she had finally decided to be a counselor. It was too bad that Tabitha figured her job out the day before I was going home. She unfolded a crumpled piece of paper. It looked like she had pulled it out of the garbage. Tabitha announced, "Um, so today, we go to breakfast. Then we have carnival prep, whatever that means. There's lunch, then siesta. After that, we go have fun at the carnival until dinner. Just a head's up: Bob is wearing stilts, so beware. His balance isn't that great."

"Thanks for the tip," Buffy said. She pulled on an orange T-shirt. It said "Bar-B-Cute" and had a picture of a smiling barbeque grill.

"Don't overdo it on the rides," Tabitha said. She was still in counselor mode. "You don't want to hurl." Tabitha held her stomach and pretended to throw up.

"Do you remember last year? One of the Chickadees ate too many cotton candies and then went on the Magic Teacup ride!" Charlie said.

"Oh my gosh, yes!" Janice said. "They had to close down the ride for an hour to clean everything up."

"What kind of rides will they have at the carnival?" Buffy asked.

"I'm pretty sure the rides haven't changed since I was a Sandpiper," Tabitha said. "They will probably have your usual suspects. There will be a Bouncy House and slides. There's probably a Ferris Wheel, a Tilt-A-Whirl, and the Pirate Ship."

"Pirate Ship" reminded me of pirate radio. It was just a few short hours away if things went according to plan. I felt a little queasy about what we were about to do. That didn't stop me from eating one of Miss Rosa's freshly baked chocolate chip muffins.

We spent our morning blowing up balloons, setting up tables, and painting signs. The afternoon siesta finally arrived. I was nervous to break the rules. I was also excited to do something for Shelby.

"Shall we?" Holly asked. She offered me her arm. She pointed in the direction of the radio station. I reluctantly hooked my arm through hers. We started walking. Tabitha was off doing something again. We didn't need a cover story for where we were going.

The door was unlocked when we got to the radio station. The studio was empty. Music played in the background. That must have been what the rest of the camp heard.

"Yessssss," Holly said in her most quiet voice.

"Clay? You in here? Hello? Anyone?" Aries asked. She looked around the studio. Clay would have answered if he had been there. Part of me wished he was there. It would not have felt like we were sneaking around if we had his help. But I highly doubt Clay would have agreed to Holly's rule-breaking plan.

"Aries, be careful," I said. I still looked around for a grown-up. Aries ignored my warning. She fiddled with the equipment. "Please don't break anything," I added. I sounded just like my mother.

"Aries, how confident are you at these controls?" Holly asked with a mischievous grin.

"Well, I've never done it on my own before," Aries said distractedly. She was still pressing buttons. "But I've watched Clay pretty closely. I'm sure I can figure it out."

"Let's fire this thing up and see what you've got," Holly said. She headed toward the sound booth. "Tara, Marla, and I will go on first, then Noodle can pop on for a couple minutes. Then the three of us will come back and close the show." Holly motioned for Tara and Marla to follow her. I just stood there in shock. Wait. What? This was exactly the same stunt Holly tried to pull on me when we were in the studio without Shelby. Darn it! Holly double-crossed me.

"But you said this show was for Noodle," Aries protested. Holly, Tara, and Marla had already put on the headphones in the sound booth and motioned that they couldn't hear Aries. Aries pressed a button and repeated herself. "This was supposed to be Noodle's show, Holly."

"And it will be," Holly said through the intercom. "In a few minutes."

"But this may not last longer than a few minutes," Aries said. This time she was a little firmer.

"Oh, come on! Relax," Holly said. "The three of us will go on first for like five minutes. Then we'll get right off the air for Noodle." Holly waved her hand at me. It was like I was some last-minute addition to her big plan. Aries crossed her arms and stopped messing with the controls.

"I didn't come all the way here to risk who-knows-what just so that you could say 'hi' to people and scream into the microphone," Aries said. She sat down with a thump on Clay's chair.

"Holly, this pirate radio stunt wasn't supposed to be about *us*. It was supposed to be *for* Shelby," I said. My cheeks burned with anger.

"For Shelby? Nuh-uh. That was your idea, Noodle. Not mine," Holly said. She showed no signs of backing down. I stared at Holly. I was furious at how she could do this to me. I wasn't sure if the other girls were stunned, or they just didn't have as much invested in pirate radio as Holly or I did. Either way, no one talked. Tara finally spoke up.

"You guys, what's more important?" she asked. She looked between Holly and me. "Sneaking onto the air like rebels or fighting with each other? I say we let Noodle go on." Now Holly looked shocked.

"I'm with Tara. Let Noodle go on," Aries said. Charlie and Janice nodded their heads. Marla looked like she would have held out longer if Tara hadn't switched sides.

"Okay, fine. Let Noodle go on," Marla said. "But we choose the music." Aries ignored her and led me up to the microphone.

"Noodle, you had better kill it on air," Holly said. She crossed her arms coldly across her chest as I walked into the booth. It only took me a moment to get settled as I put on some headphones.

"Aries, can you track the time for me? Give me five minutes with a one-minute warning. I don't think we'll get that much time, but who knows?" I asked. I pulled out the material I had rewritten. My heart pounded in my chest. I took a deep breath as I watched Aries press some buttons. *This is who you wanted to be*, I reminded myself. The programmed music shut off. Aries held up her fingers and counted down from three to one. She signaled that I was live on the air.

"Good afternoon, Camp Hillside. This is Noodle Newman coming to you with a special edition of Radio Hillside. We'll call it Pirate Radio Hillside," I began. "Listen up, campers! We're probably breaking a million rules here. But the Sandpipers have not always followed the rules." Aries gave me a thumbs-up from the control room. The other girls watched me from outside the studio. They pressed their faces up to the glass window.

"You got this," Charlie mouthed. Tara waved her hands in the air. I could feel my confidence growing as I continued.

"I want to give a special shout-out to our counselor, Shelby St. James. She had to leave Camp Hillside a few weeks ago," I said. I barely looked at my notes. "I had a pretty miserable start to camp, but I stayed because of Shelby," I said. I looked at my bunkmates. They listened closely. I wondered if anyone else around camp heard us. It was hard to tell from a booth with no windows. "Shelby, I know you're not listening. But I just want you to know that you inspired me. I wish you could see how much I have changed over these past four weeks."

"I would also like to thank Hurricane Hilda for shaking things up a bit," I continued. "Without the storm, we never would have been stuck indoors without power for four days. The Sandpipers became friends because of that crazy situation. We've gone through a lot together. We had a change in counselors. Our cabin flooded. We did some terrible pranks. We ate enough cold cereal to last a lifetime. I'm going to miss you girls. I'm glad that we made so many great memories together." Aries gave me the one-minute warning. I motioned for the girls to come into the booth with me. Marla was the first to race in. I guess she wasn't annoyed anymore.

Charlie, Janice, Buffy, and Tara quickly followed her. They crowded into the cramped room with me. Holly stayed put. I waved furiously for her to join, too.

"Oh my gosh! This is crazy!" Janice shrieked. She was unable to contain herself. "I can't believe we're on air!"

"I thought we should end this pirate radio broadcast with the Sandpiper's own version of our camp song, 'Forever Hillside.' In honor of Shelby," I said. "Girls, give me your left-left, your left-right-left. On my count!" "Forever Hillside" was about our love for the colors green and yellow. It was about the wind blowing in the hills. It helped us to remember our friends, both near and far. We even added in a special verse about the Sandpipers that we had made up with Shelby. We put our arms around each other and swayed as we sang together. We were probably very off-key, but we didn't really care.

"Noodle, you close out the show," Holly said. She gently patted my back. I nodded and turned back to the microphone.

"Signing off from Radio Hillside, I'm Noodle Newman, and these are my fellow Sandpipers for life." I heard something outside the glass. I looked at Aries. Then I saw an angry-looking Bob and Dotty and a confused Clay run into the control room. "I think we're in pretty big trouble now," I added. I pulled off my headphones. I wasn't sure if we were even on the air anymore.

Chapter 22

BOB AND DOTTY'S VERDICT

"What in the dickens do you think you're doing?" Bob sputtered. His red face looked even redder against his white hair. "Sneaking onto the air? What has gotten into you girls?"

All I could think was, *Boy, they got to the studio fast.* Nobody said a word. We tried to avoid eye contact with Bob and Dotty.

"The carnival is about to start. Dotty and I don't have time to deal with this . . . *incident* right now," Bob sputtered. His tone was as angry as a clap of thunder.

"Go to your cabin until further notice," Dotty commanded. Her eyes blazed with fury. "*Straight* to your cabin. Tabitha is waiting for you there." We slowly shuffled back to our cabin. We passed by the huge carnival that we had helped set up.

"It sure looks fun," Buffy said sadly. She read my mind. She was wearing her yellow "Girls Just Wanna Have Sun" T-shirt today in honor of the carnival. It was a shame that we had to be stuck inside now.

"You guys, it's just a carnival," Holly scoffed. "If you've been to one, you've been to 'em all."

"But this one has unlimited cotton candy," Marla said. She pointed to the line of campers waiting for an oversized cone.

"My parents aren't here to tell me I can only have one." We all trudged along silently. Everyone had their own reasons for why missing the carnival would stink.

"Look! Those are the Sandpipers!" I heard a few of the campers exclaim as we walked by. "They just snuck on the radio."

"They're going to get in big trouble for sure," a little girl said. Aries glanced at the girl and shot her a dirty look. As we straggled up the hill, Tabitha whistled to us from the front steps of our bunk.

"You guys really did it this time," Tabitha said with a cackle. When she saw our glum faces, Tabitha softened her tone. "Listen 'Pipers, I did some dumb things at camp when I was your age. Nothing this dumb, of course . . . but I give you a ton of credit for being so bold. I definitely didn't think you had it in you after your other failed pranks." she added.

"Hey, Tabitha," I said. I tried to change the subject. "What would you do now if you were in our shoes? How would you get out of being punished?" Tabitha looked at me in a way that almost seemed respectful. It was as if she had suddenly found her purpose as our counselor.

"Dotty and Bob are your aunt and uncle, so you probably know them better than anyone else," Aries offered. She caught my eye with a slight nod.

"Hmmm," she said after a moment. "That's a very interesting question. What *would* I do?" Tabitha paced around the cabin, deep in thought.

"Well, Aunt Dotty and Uncle Bob are big softies at heart. And you've got that underdog thing going for you, Noodle," Tabitha said. She grew more animated. "We've got to use that to our advantage." *We?* I thought. I tried not to show my surprise.

"I wish I knew how I could get us out of this mess," I said. My eyes welled up with tears. "I'm sorry, you guys."

"Hopefully, Bob and Dotty will go easy on all of you," Tabitha offered. She gave me a tissue that she fished out of her bag. I nodded. At this point, there was nothing else to do but wait.

Kurt the Flirt and another swim instructor (who was just as handsome) hand-delivered us a tray of hot dogs and cotton candy. Then Bob and Dotty came up to the cabin to issue our punishment.

"We know that tonight is the last night at camp for some of you," Bob began. He looked at Buffy, Marla, and me. "It's unfortunate that you've now missed the carnival due to your . . . stunt."

"This type of behavior will not be tolerated at Camp Hillside today or in the future," Dotty said. She seemed even angrier than before.

"Aunt Dotty, Uncle Bob, could I say a few words?" Tabitha interrupted. We were shocked.

"Why yes, Tabitha dear. Go ahead," Dotty said. She looked confused. Her tone softened.

"I think these young ladies have realized that they've made a terrible mistake," Tabitha began. She used that same fake voice we heard the night we first met her. "They were reckless.

They behaved in a manner that was unbecoming of Hillside girls. They put the great Camp Hillside name at risk." Bob and Dotty stared at her closely. So did the rest of us.

"Where is she going with this?" Aries whispered to me. I shrugged. I couldn't take my eyes off Tabitha.

"But I have spent a lot of time with the Sandpipers over the past several weeks. I know that these campers care deeply for each other," Tabitha said. She looked straight into Bob and Dotty's eyes. "They have been through so much this summer. They lost their beloved counselor, Shelby. The storm ruined their cabin. They have faced so many challenges. But they have overcome each obstacle together, as Sandpipers."

Bob and Dotty still seemed pretty mad. But I could also see something else on their faces. They looked proud of Tabitha. I wanted to believe that Tabitha's words made everything okay. But I couldn't take that chance. I knew *I* had to do something.

"Um, Dotty? Bob? Can I also say something?" I asked. My voice was shaking. "I, uh, wanted to tell you that pirate radio was . . . uh . . . my fault." The rest of the cabin gasped. "I really wanted to go back on the air before I went home. I couldn't wait until next summer. I am so sorry for my behavior, and I will accept any punishment on behalf of all the Sandpipers."

"Noodle, no!" Aries said. Her eyes filled with tears. "You can't do that!" The rest of the girls protested that I shouldn't take the blame. Holly just looked at me. She didn't say a word.

"Ladies, give us a moment to discuss these . . . latest statements," Dotty said. She motioned for Bob to follow her outside.

"Of course," Tabitha said. She stood next to me. "Take your time."

Tabitha patted my shoulder as soon as Bob and Dotty left. "Nice touch, Noodle."

"I meant it," I said. Tabitha waved me off and stared out the window. She drummed her fingers on the windowsill. No one had the energy to tell her to stop. I flopped face-down on my bed. How long would it take for Bob and Dotty to come back? What were they going to do to me? After a few minutes, I felt a tap on my foot. I jerked my leg without thinking.

"Ow, Noodle!" I saw Holly standing at the foot of my bed when I looked up.

"I'm so sorry," I said. "I thought you were a spider or something."

"Listen, I just wanted to tell you that what you did . . . offering to take the blame for us and all . . . well, that was really cool," Holly said. She walked away before I could respond. She turned so quickly that her ponytail swished back and forth. It was like it was nodding and telling me that it also agreed.

It felt like hours before Bob and Dotty returned. It had probably been about ten minutes before they came back inside with their news. Bob cleared his throat to get our attention.

"Because of the unfortunate timing of this incident, Tabitha's moving speech, and Noodle's . . . offer," Bob began. He glanced at Tabitha and me. I sat on my hands and held my breath. "Tomorrow, at sunrise, *all* of the Sandpipers must raise the flag for reveille."

"But reveille is sooo early," Marla whined.

"Shhh!" Holly said. She glared at Marla. Maybe Marla's complaint was just for show. The punishment didn't seem all that bad. And it wasn't just for me!

"In the future," Dotty continued in her serious voice. "We cannot promise that we will go easy on you for violations of this sort. Are we clear?"

"Crystal!" we shouted together. I definitely shouted the loudest.

"Good. It's time for Shower Hour," Bob said. "We'll see you at dinner." We erupted in cheers when Bob and Dotty had left.

"Tabitha, you really saved us!" I said. "Thank you for what you said. Shelby would have been proud." I could've sworn I saw a tear well up in Tabitha's eye.

"Aw shucks, Noodle. You aren't too shabby yourself," Tabitha said. "Hey, if you ever write a book or something, make sure you make me a good character."

"Deal," I said. I wasn't sure I could deliver on that promise. A little while later, Tabitha reappeared for dinner. After all the excitement that afternoon, I was starving.

"Ladies, grab a sweatshirt . . . and some bug spray. Dinner is waiting for you up *there*," Tabitha said. She pointed up the hill instead of down toward the Mess Hall.

"I wonder what they're serving tonight," Buffy asked. She broke our stunned silence. Her T-shirt had a picture of a chocolate chip cookie wearing boxing gloves. I knew that it said "One Tough Cookie" without even reading the caption. For my birthday, I would definitely ask for a gift card to the store where Buffy bought her shirts.

As we walked, campers who would have normally just passed us by pointed in our direction and whispered, "Look, it's the Sandpipers!"

"Your pirate radio show rocked," a random camper said. She gave Aries and me a high-five.

"Can't wait for you to go back on Radio Hillside again, whichever one of you is Noodle!" one girl said as she passed.

"I couldn't have done it without Aries! She's my partner at the controls," I said. I gestured to Aries. Her smile radiated from deep inside her.

"We make a great team," Aries said after the girls had passed. I gasped at the amazing sight at the top of the hill. There was an enormous bonfire and a huge grill. My nostrils were greeted by the delicious smell of chicken. My stomach grumbled.

Dinner was one of my new favorites: chicken kebabs. The sign by the kebabs said "KeBobs" and had a funny picture of Bob holding chicken skewers. I put two KeBobs on my very full plate.

I thought about my twenty-seven days at camp as I ate. I might have found my footing sooner if I had had a better idea of what to expect. Jill had told me plenty of stories, but those stories didn't mean anything until I came to camp on my own. I wish I could go back in time and tell myself that I would be okay. This gave me a great idea. I pulled out my trusty notepad. I jotted down one final letter. This time, I wrote to myself.

Dear Pre-camp Noodle,

Trust me when I tell you that you will do just fine at camp. If you don't want to waste too much time feeling sad, here's what you will have to do right off the bat:

1. Get over being homesick as soon as you can. You have the courage and strength inside of you already; find it as fast as you can so you don't miss too much!

2. Make friends with at least one or two nice kids. Look harder if you don't find them immediately. Good friends will help you through tough times.

3. Have fun, but keep out of trouble. Stay on all the paths, don't take shortcuts down any hills, and don't leave food—or clothing with food on it—outside your cabin.

4. Last but not least, don't do anything _too_ crazy. Hopefully you'll know how far you should go!

You can thank me later for all the tissues that I've just saved you.

Love, Noodle

P.S. Don't drink the bug juice. It's never going to taste as good as you think it should.

Just as I had finished my letter, Miss Rosa announced that the dessert station was ready. It was my other new favorite food: s'mores! I put away my notebook and ran toward the line that was forming near the graham crackers. What an amazing night!

The mosquitoes really started to bite when the fire died down. It was time to head back to our cabins. Several of the girls linked arms. They wanted to hold onto the spirit of Camp Hillside a little longer. We walked along in a happy silence. Tara and Holly chanted another one of their silly camp rhymes. They never seemed to run out. "Potato chips, potato chips, *munch munch munch*! We think the Sandpipers are a mighty fine bunch!"

The Goldfinches echoed the cheer. They said, "Goldfinches" instead of "Sandpipers."

"Those girls need some new material," Buffy joked. She pointed at Holly and Tara and shook her head. We felt an amazing sense of friendship as our two cabins walked together. *This was such a special night*, I thought. *I should write every-thing down as soon as I get back. I don't want to forget a moment of it.* But when we got back to our cabin, I laid down. I put my head down on my pillow and fell fast asleep.

Chapter 23

GOODBYE FOR NOW

Tabitha grouchily woke us up at the crack of dawn on Sunday morning. We soon realized our punishment was a blessing in disguise.

"I never knew that the sunrise could be so beautiful," Janice said. She hugged her knees to her chest. She stared at the bright blue sky.

"I see a cloud over there. We should probably go back to bed," Marla said with a yawn. "You guys! Can you pull up the flag a little quicker?" The cabin had volunteered Holly and Tara to raise the flag as payback for their failed pranks.

"When I got to camp, I couldn't wait for today to come," I said to Charlie. "Now I'm sad that today is finally here." She smiled and gave my arm a gentle squeeze.

"Next year will be even better," she whispered. She grabbed Aries' and my hand as we went to breakfast. *This will be my last chocolate chip muffin from Miss Rosa*, I thought. Maybe she would give me the recipe. I wanted to make them at home with my mom. I tried to savor every bite as I looked around the Mess Hall. I already felt nostalgic.

I went back to the cabin after breakfast to finish packing up my things. Buffy and Marla stuffed their trunks with dirty clothes. We didn't notice the rest of the girls quietly walk in.

"Good. You're all here," Holly announced loudly. I nearly dropped what I was packing up. "I'm calling to order our *second* unofficial cabin meeting." We hurried over to the dusty braided rug. This old rug held years of laughter and memories. Now it had mine.

"Noodle, Buffy, Marla," Holly said seriously. "You guys are really special to this cabin. We decided to make you all a memory book." Tara proudly handed a slim book to each of us.

"We didn't have a lot of time to work on it, and the printer in the main office got jammed. Then it ran out of paper. Then Marjorie told us we had to leave . . . so there's not a lot there," Janice said. She shrugged her shoulders sheepishly.

"Thick or thin, we wanted you to have something to help you remember your time as a Sandpiper," Charlie said. "We all signed it like a yearbook," she said. She grabbed Marla's book and flipped through a few pages to show us.

"We're really going to miss you guys," Tara said. She wiped a tear away. Aries didn't speak. She just nodded quietly.

"The rest of the summer won't be the same without you," Aries said. She wrapped me in a hug. I hugged her back even harder and felt the tears well up in my eyes. This time, they were happy tears. I tried not to get too emotional because I only had one tissue left. I would have to wait until my mother and her never-ending tissue supply arrived. After I tucked my last soggy tissue into my pocket, I tried to close my trunk. I had packed and repacked everything. I couldn't get the latch to close no matter how hard I tried. *How did everything fit the first time?* I wondered. My parents would arrive any minute now and I still had a few more goodbyes.

"Here, let me help you," Aries said as she climbed on top of my trunk. Even though a shirt sleeve still poked out, we managed to shut the lid before Aries fell off.

"Teamwork!" we both shouted at the same time. We high-fived happily. As I tested the lock on my trunk again, I heard a familiar voice.

"There she is!" the voice boomed. I would recognize my father's voice anywhere.

"My little girl! Oh, look at you!" my mother said as she ran into the cabin. She nearly knocked my dad over. I blushed with embarrassment. "You look so skinny. Have you been eating?" My mother looked at me with concern.

"Mom! Dad!" I said as my mother smothered me with kisses. After a moment, I pulled away. "I want you to meet my friend, Aries." Aries was just about to sneak out of the cabin. She stuck out her hand awkwardly to my dad.

"Nice to meet you, sir, er, doctor," Aries said in a strangely formal voice.

"So, this is the famous Aries," my father said warmly. "Thanks for looking after Noodle. We're lucky she met you."

"The feeling is mutual," Aries answered. Aries was still Aries, though, and small talk wasn't her strong suit. Before she slipped out, she whispered, "This isn't goodbye for us, right?"

"Of course not," I said. "We'll write and we'll call each other. Plus, you don't live that far from Great Falls. You're only a train ride away." I wasn't sure my parents would let me take the train to Aries' house by myself, but my birthday was at the end of August. Who knew what might happen next year?

"You better keep in touch or else," Aries said softly. She sniffled. We hugged one more time before Aries pulled away.

"Well, I'll let you get your things together," Aries said seriously. She quickly excused herself. "It was nice meeting you Dr. and Mrs. Newman. Noodle really made camp a not-so-terrible experience for me this summer."

"That's a compliment," I whispered.

"Well, that's, um . . . fantastic to hear," my mom answered. She wasn't sure how to respond.

"Goodbyes aren't my thing, so . . . I'll see you later, Noodle," Aries said. She hurried out the door. I saw her wipe her eyes with her shirt. I knew how hard this must be for her. I smiled sadly as my best camp friend disappeared.

I had said goodbye to everyone at least twice. I had not said goodbye to Tabitha. She was missing once again. She didn't seem like the type who said goodbye anyway.

"I think I'm going to get a hernia from lifting this thing," my dad teased as he tried to pick up my trunk. I had missed my dad's sense of humor.

"I know a guy who can help with that. He owes me," I said. Kurt the Flirt would surely help. There was no swim class today. I took one more long look around the cabin. I gave Charlie and Janice one last hug before I went outside.

As my parents and I walked down the hill to our car, I saw a dark figure waving at us.

"Noodle Newman, were you trying to leave this camp without saying goodbye?" Tabitha asked in a way that I soon realized was her joking.

"Of course not," I said. "But I couldn't find you after reveille. I looked everywhere!"

"Well, I have even more work to do now. My aunt and uncle asked me to help out in the Arts and Crafts Studio," Tabitha said. "It's sort of like my second home. Anyway, I'll mail you some watercolor paintings that I did this summer. I painted some great still lifes of the hills and the Great Lake."

"Painting? Huh. I never knew," I said. I was surprised by the revelation of Tabitha's secret. Tabitha had been sneaking off to the Arts and Crafts Studio all this time.

"See you back here next year, Noodle?" Tabitha asked. I looked at my parents and nodded. "Between you and me," Tabitha whispered loudly as she softly poked me in the ribs, "my aunt and uncle could really use your help in the entertainment department."

I smiled and said in an equally loud whisper, "I know."

"Oh, hey, before you go. Shelby wanted me to give this to you," Tabitha said. She handed me an intricately woven friendship bracelet. "I forgot to give it to you sooner. I found it this morning when I was cleaning out my bag."

"Thank you. Wow, it's so cool!" I exclaimed. I admired it on my wrist. "Better late than never. I love it."

"Well, stay out of trouble if you can, Noodle Newman," Tabitha said with a wave. She walked away. I waved back at Tabitha. I might even miss her too, but only a little bit.

Jill once told me that "the diehard campers all live 'ten for two.' They wait for ten months out of the year for the two months of summer." Now I understood what she meant. I knew things wouldn't be the same for me at Camp Hillside next summer. But next year I knew I wouldn't have to relive the homesickness. I walked with my parents to our car and realized that this really was just "goodbye for now." As I walked down the hill, I hummed softly to myself, "Give me your left-left, your left-right-left," and smiled.

ACKNOWLEDGMENTS

To Joan and Larry Cohen, for being such amazing characters in every way. Thank you for all your love and encouragement, and for humoring my various childhood artistic expressions. Although you've given me so much over the years, the greatest gift I have ever received was your DNA.

To Andrea Kaiser, for being the most fantastic big sister, role model, and best friend. Craig, Stella, Milly, and Lulu are lucky to have you in their lives. It isn't too late to add them as honorary members of the Pruss Club.

To Jennifer Rees, Tamson Weston, and Amy Hest for your spot-on editing advice. I am incredibly grateful for your insights and feedback, even though I wished the writing process required fewer rounds of revisions.

To my friends, both past and present, for their support, kindness, and advice. Thanks for never asking "what's taking you so long to finish your book?"

To all the teachers who fostered my creativity. A special thank you to those educators who saw promise in me despite my terrible handwriting.

To my early readers, for their time and feedback. Your enthusiasm made me feel like a celebrity, but without the hassle of any paparazzi.

To my darling children, Rafael and Simon. You give me the inspiration to continue doing what I love. Now that you are both old enough to read my books, I welcome your plot and character suggestions.

And, finally, to my beloved husband Roy. Your vision and confidence in all things (including me) are an inspiration. Thank you for giving me the courage to follow the dreams of my eight-year-old self. As they say in fishing, you're a keeper.

ABOUT THE AUTHOR

In third grade, Steph Katzovi announced that she was going to be author when she grew up.

Realizing that she might want to explore other career options first, Steph got her bachelor's degree from Binghamton University before attending Brooklyn Law School. Although she aced the legal writing classes and wrote amazing outlines for exams, Steph knew her calling was not as a practicing attorney. After graduation, Steph shelved her law degree and two bar admissions to become a professional writer. She spent the bulk of her fifteen-plus year career at Deloitte as a speechwriter and strategic communications consultant. When the opportunity arose to raise her children and focus more fully on creative writing, Steph decided it was time to take her "When I Grow Up" essay from third grade a bit more seriously.

If she's not busy writing at her desk in New York City, Steph is a sports and exercise enthusiast. She also enjoys playing guitar and piano with her two sons, going out on date nights with her husband, and reading—preferably poolside.